MW00937580

Desolation Sound

FRASER C. HESTON
AND
HEATHER J. MCADAMS

Published by Agamemnon Films
650 N. Bronson Ave. B225
Los Angeles, CA 90004
www.agamemnon.com
www.desolationsoundnovel.com

ISBN-13: 9781514193945
ISBN-10: 1514193949

Book cover design by Hakon Envig
Photo by Fraser C. Heston

How often have I said to you that when you have eliminated the impossible, then whatever remains, however improbable, *must be the truth?*

~ Sir Arthur Conan Doyle
The Sign of Four

1

A man slices through dark water, knifes powerfully the blade of his paddle, cutting into the smoothly yielding, oily surface of the sea, pulling the kayak along with each powerful stroke, surging ahead toward a not too distant shore. Beyond the rocky beach ahead, cut by the mouth of a small stream, waits a dark line of dripping conifers, heavy with rain and Spanish moss, growing right out of tidewater, marking a ragged ridgeline on the island. Behind that rises a line of hazy blue mountains still patched with snow, glowing faintly pink from the sun still hidden behind the rim of the world. Remote, unobtainable, mysterious in their way, these peaks, as if they were in Tibet though they are in fact only on Vancouver Island. The man will never go to Tibet, nor to the peaks before him. He must be content with these islands.

The man's name is Jack Harris. He was once a policeman. A detective. No longer. That's all behind him. Like the slippery wake of his kayak, disappearing into the murky water.

A sudden breath rises from the sea, also somewhere behind him, a sort of small explosion throwing off his stroke, making the fly rod strapped to the foredeck bungees quiver. Probably a sea lion, he thinks. Sometimes they would follow him as he paddled along through these islands, curious. Sliding beside him a few feet under the water, gazing up at him with big dark eyes. He usually enjoyed the company. But this morning he would find company of another kind.

Another breath, louder, closer. And then another—bigger and more powerful—and the man's stroke falters, he digs one paddle blade in and leans on it hard, putting the kayak on its chine, stepping hard on the rudder pedal and turning the boat in a short smooth arc. Looks back.

Another whoosh and a tall black fin leaps out of the sea behind him, simultaneously with another exhalation, leaving hardly a splash. *Booosh!* Then another and another and another and then the tall majestic black fin again, six feet high, slicing through the sea like the conning tower of a submarine surfacing and coming inexorably for him. A big male.

Jack knows where the orcas are headed: a small rocky islet at the head of the bay he calls simply Sea Lion Island—because it's covered at most times with a large colony of barking, smelly Steller sea lions, which also happen to be the favorite food of orcas. He sits bobbing in his kayak, watching the tall dorsals and misting spouts come closer; he's directly on a line between the whales and their prey. He does not feel particularly threatened, he knows he's not on their usual menu and orcas as a rule do not attack men in small boats, and in any case there is little he can do.

Still his heart pounds up into his throat as they approach, blowing hard now and sounding one last time, the tall fins knifing through the glassy dark green water and angling sharply downward as the whales sound. He wishes he'd had time to get his cell phone out for a photo—surely they would surface right beside him. But it is not to be—he feels a faint surge in the water beneath him as they pass, submerged. He can distinctly see the large white patches on the orcas' flanks as they glide effortlessly by, one of the big males turning a large, calm, baleful eye upon him, ancient and somehow very wise, and then they are gone. Only surfacing after some time about a hundred yards down the bay. Jack realizes he has been holding his breath and lets it out unsteadily, his hands only now beginning to shake, digs the paddle into the water to make his way toward the mouth of the little creek.

Jack sees some commotion over toward Sea Lion Island, as the sea lions realize what nightmare has descended upon their world and in their panic begin to bark and gallop and flop into the sea, of all places, right into the path of the now-encircling flanks of the killer whale pod, which has divided into two groups on either side of the rock and comes surging hard and fast up into the herd of sea lions with a great splashing of white water . . . then silence, save for the barking of the panicked survivors, a few crying gulls wheeling after scraps. Jack cannot see blood in the water but knows it is there.

■ ■ ■

Jack paddles hard and the little kayak slides easily up the shingle of the gravel beach near the creek mouth. He clambers stiffly out of the cockpit, steps into the shallow water in his black gumboots, drags the kayak up well above the water line. He unstraps the fly rod from the deck bungees, puts the small box of hand-tied sea-run cutthroat flies, surprisingly delicate and traditional-looking little creatures, into his anorak pocket, and walks down the beach, stripping off some line. He wades out a little ways and begins to false cast. He starts well up in the current of the creek, working out about thirty or forty feet of line in tight narrow loops and drops a cast above the mouth of the creek. He mends the line slightly upstream and lets the current carry the fly downstream and across under slight tension, the line bowing into a *J* shape, waiting for the strong subtle tug at the end of the swing, which does not come. He gives the line a twitch or two and strips in slowly, moves two steps downstream and repeats the process, each time casting out effortlessly, the unfurling tight-looped line sending droplets of spray over the slick water, catching the sunlight, swinging his fly down and across, two-stepping down with the current as if he were steelhead fishing. *Perhaps they are not running today*, he thinks. *Or perhaps I need to change flies.*

As he works downstream toward the mouth of the creek, Jack notices something half-buried in the pea gravel at the high-tide mark among the wrack of seaweed and driftwood. Something man-made. It is a running shoe of some sort, partially buried upside down in the gravel, its white cushy rubber sole picked out in the sunlight, strangely out of place in this pristine natural world, vaguely offensive to Jack's aesthetic. He pokes it with the butt of his rod. It is pretty well buried and does not dislodge readily; he gives it a good shove with his boot and the shoe turns over and inside the shoe is a human foot.

Jack can clearly see the smooth anklebone protruding from a ragged edge of flesh and stringy sinew, pale as the sole of the shoe, which is slimed with green algae but not barnacles. It has not been in the water long enough for barnacles to grow. The gray sock is bunched around the ankle. He squats by the shoe, looks at it closely. He cannot tell how the foot had been severed, but he can see where sea creatures— shrimps, prawns and crabs perhaps—had begun to work on it, gnawing away with ragged mindless patience in some bathymetric darkness, before the foot floated free and washed ashore.

He takes out his cell phone—he has one bar—and tries 911. Astonishingly, he gets through after a couple of rings.

"Nine-one-one, Emergency. What is the nature of your emergency, please?"

"I'd like to report a human foot."

"I'm sorry sir, can you repeat that?"

"A severed foot, severed human foot, in a running shoe, washed up on the shore of Valdes Island, here in the Gulf Islands. Right across from Francisco Island."

"Is anyone injured? Are you injured, sir? Was this an accident?"

No, he was not injured, he had no idea if it was an accident, and no, there was no one hobbling around missing a foot. No body, either alive or dead, that he could see, that could match up with this foot. Eventually he makes the operator understand what he has found and gives her the coordinates of the island and the creek mouth, in as much detail as he can, and agrees to hang around until the authorities show up. He gives her his cell number and hangs up, settling in to wait. He knows it will be a while.

It is. Jack takes the little stainless-steel flask out of his jacket, and has a nip of the Macallan, just a wee morning nip to warm his heart and steady his slightly unsettled nerves, the long, smooth burning slug of it dropping into his bones, the first of the day, and it is good. He needed that. No one likes finding body parts first thing in the morning. On impulse, he takes a picture of the foot with his cell phone, from several angles, one quite close, and notes the time. Time is always important in such matters. He sits on a driftwood log for a while, staring out at Sea Lion Island, but the killer whales and the sea lions have gone, doing whatever it is they do when they are not killing or being eaten. He gets tired of that after an hour or so and thinks what the hell he might as well go fishing. He bites off the fly, sticks it in his baseball cap and ties on a small sparse brown-gray muddler minnow, one of the great all-purpose flies of all time. He casts out a few more times and hooks a nice sea-run cutthroat, it fights hard for a bit and pulls out some line from the reel, and eventually comes smoothly to hand, nearly eighteen inches, lying gasping in the shallow water, the distinctive blood-red mark beneath its jaw which gives the fish its name showing clearly. Jack slips out the hook and releases it, watches it swim into the limpid green depths and disappear.

2

Kneeling on the Stanley Park seawall at the start of a running trail, a striking blonde clad in Under Armour tights and a fitted spandex top tightens up the laces on her running shoes, her breath frosting in the brisk morning air. She sports a Bluetooth headset and a black paracord bracelet. She sets off at an easy running pace through the forest, blond hair glistening in the shafts of sunlight slanting through the trees. Liz MacDonald finds solace in her solitary runs. She is good at running. Fast, graceful gait. She likes how her lungs burn in the cold air. How her mind can wander and not have to think about anything but the rhythmic sounds her feet make in the fallen leaves. No-mind: a form of meditation.

It's a beautiful, cool morning, mist rising through the heavy timber cut by bands of sunlight. Stanley Park, essentially an island in Vancouver Harbour connected to the mainland and the city of Vancouver by a narrow isthmus at one end and the majestic span of Lion's Gate Bridge on the other, is a green oasis with a seawall encircling a thousand acres of giant old-growth cedars, hiking and biking trails, a small lake, the Vancouver Aquarium and a cricket pitch. In the middle of the park, there is a wild solitary calm camouflaging the proximity of a major downtown metropolis—a tiny remnant of the great conifer forest which once stretched from Big Sur to Alaska and now survives only in small showpiece forests like Stanley Park.

Other joggers on the path nod hello as they pass. Liz catches up and passes one woman, pleased that she has a nice pace working. She hears footsteps behind her. She doesn't want anyone to pass her, so she kicks it up a notch. She glances over her shoulder and sees a man in black, a dark figure jogging fifty yards behind her through the trees. His pace matching hers. She picks it up another notch, and so does he. Just to test him, she slows down to let him pass, but he doesn't.

Mildly concerned, Liz quickens her pace over a wooden footbridge to see if he follows suit. The man runs faster, feet clumping over the wooden bridge. She ducks into a narrow side trail between old-growth cedars. She can no longer hear his footsteps; she seems to have shaken him. But as she turns back toward the main trail, the man tackles her to the ground. She hits hard, biting her lip and skinning her knee. She rolls onto her back and kicks out, connecting with something soft. The man drops onto her, pinning her to the ground, fumbling at her breasts, her crotch. The man pulls out a pre-looped zip tie from his pocket and tries to get it over her hands.

The man snarls through clenched teeth, "Come on sweetheart, this is what you really want."

It sends an electric surge of adrenaline through her body; Liz adroitly fends him off, kicking up her legs and flipping him over.

"RCMP, you're under arrest!" she yells. But it has no effect. Another scuffle—she tries to get handcuffs on him—he fights back hard. A desperate struggle in the dirt, an ineffectual wrestling match Liz manages to call on her Bluetooth, "I've got him! Get in here now! Officer needs assistance!"

■ ■ ■

Her backup partners, two plainclothes detectives, Frank Richards and Doug Fouché, are sitting nearby in an un-marked car, drinking coffee. Richards has the look of someone who let himself go after he started losing his hair, perhaps figuring that once the hair goes, inevitably the rest follows. The years of bad food, alcohol, stress and ciga-rettes are catching up with him. His younger counterpart, on the other hand, is religious about working out and what he eats. He's the guy with the green drink and perfectly balanced carb-protein ratios. Eager to please. Quick to attention, as soon as Fouché hears Liz, he jumps out of the car, but Richards stops him.

"What's your rush? Let's season the rookie a little."

"Season her? Are you kidding? She needs backup."

Richards takes a drag on his cigarette. "She won't always have backup."

Uncertain, Fouché hesitates by the car. "Fuck that." He then starts down the trail at a trot.

Richards smiles, takes a drag on his cigarette and follows.

■ ■ ■

Liz struggles with her assailant on the ground. He pulls her ponytail and she whips around and punches him in the neck. He releases his grip and she tries to handcuff him.

"I am arresting you for assault and attempted rape. You have the right to retain and instruct counsel—"

But then he gets an arm loose; he finds a heavy stick and hits her hard, opening up a cut above her left eye. Breaking free, he runs. She sprints after him, tackles him, takes the stick away. She finishes reading him his rights as she tries to secure both handcuffs.

"You are not obliged to say anything, but anything you do say may be given in evidence."

The man flips his head back hard into her nose. Liz is momentarily stunned and the man begins to wriggle free.

Reflexively, she grabs the discarded stick and hits him hard on the side of the head and finishes cuffing him.

"Would you like to speak to a lawyer now, you sonofabitch?"

■ ■ ■

Fouché shows up just as the perp, now battered and bleeding from several cuts, is subdued. Richards pants up from behind, gasping. Liz wipes the blood off her forehead.

Fouché pulls the perp from the ground, braces him against a tree and pats him down. He removes his cell phone and pockets it.

"Nice job, MacDonald " says Richards.

"Nice job? Where the hell were you?"

Fouché covers, "Ah . . . sorry, we got lost in the woods."

Liz stares them both down. "You're a prince among men."

Richards chuckles as he picks up the discarded stick. "You see Fouché, she doesn't speak softly but still carries the big stick."

3

Liz watches Richards and Fouché interrogate the suspect from Stanley Park through a two-way mirror. Liz wasn't asked to be a part of the interrogation because her official position is RCMP Media Liaison or as the guys in her division call her, "the PR Gal." When the Stanley Park Rapist revealed a pattern of going after runners, Liz had volunteered for the honey trap. An opportunity to break free of being the pretty face and PR spokesperson on TV. Liz wanted to make her mark.

The RCMP provides both national and provincial police protection to Canada. An unimaginably huge territory, but indeed the Mounties usually get their man. Some say the aphorism is based on Canadians' natural tenacity and perseverance, while others believe it dates back to the 1870s, when it was reported that the Mounties were like bloodhounds when tracking whiskey smugglers. Once they got on the scent of a smuggler, they always got their man. Every time. Liz daydreamed of being that kind of a Mountie when she was a little girl.

Liz nervously sips her coffee. She looks over the case file labeled TIMMONS, WILLIAM and then back at the interrogation room. Timmons is an oddly attractive thirty-something with a cool demeanor. He appears unfazed by the sudden turn of events in his day. He looks like a regular guy.

What turns someone into a sexual predator? Liz wonders. *People have the misconception that only unattractive people rape. People who couldn't get laid otherwise commit this act. But sexual frustration has nothing to do with it. Not really. It's an act of violence, a rage that is inside some men. Rage that builds up over time after an unhappy childhood, possible suffering from abuse or neglect along with some bad wiring in their brains.* Liz wants to put this one away. *Seven victims and counting.*

Richards looks at Timmons directly. "State your name and address please."

Timmons meets Richards' stare. Touches the makeshift bandage on his head. "William Timmons. 3151 Alberta Street, Vancouver V781S5."

"Are you employed?"

"Yes. I work for Vancouver Animal Control. Before that, I served as a medic with the Princess Pats in Afghanistan. We're basically on the same side."

Fouché scoffs, "Not quite. You tried to rape another girl today."

Timmons is silent and stares straight ahead.

Richards slams down victim photos, trying to get a re-action. The photos are an array of bruised and bloodied women. Some have finger-shaped bruising around their necks. One girl's eye is swollen shut above a bloodied lip. Sad, flat eyes stare into the camera. Shattered life after a morning run.

"Just like the seven other girls you stalked, assaulted, beat and raped."

Timmons glances at the photos. No response.

Liz jots down notes. Was there a hint of arousal? Of recognition?

Timmons pushes the photos back to Richards. "These are horrible photos. I hope you find the person who did this."

"What were you doing in Stanley Park?"

"Jogging."

"Why were you following Corporal MacDonald?"

"I was jogging on the same trail when she tackled me, beat me up and arrested me for no reason."

"You had condoms in your wallet and zip ties in your pocket."

"Oh my goodness! Condoms? There's a crime!"

"That's a traveling rape kit."

Timmons smiles, shrugs. "I'm a single guy and I use zip ties for my job."

"I thought you were out for a jog?"

Fouché plays good cop. "Look. I know how women can be. They run ahead and taunt you. MacDonald is a hot little number. She probably deserved it."

"Your hot little number better get a lawyer. I'm suing for police brutality and entrapment. Now, I want my lawyer." Timmons smiles. "And . . . proper medical attention."

Liz slams her notebook shut.

4

Jack is casting again when he finally hears the big RIB Zodiac approaching from down the sound. He feels a bit guilty about being caught fishing in such grave circumstance, but it's been a couple of hours and not fishing wouldn't help whomever it was who had lost the foot at this point. Eventually two uniformed RCMP constables approach in their inflatable and land on the beach wearing thick, navy blue float-coats with reflective patches.

"Good day, sir. Are you Jack Harris, called about a body part washed ashore near here?" The voice sounds unnaturally harsh and loud in this quiet reverential place.

"Good day to you, constable. I am. Just over here."

"May we see some ID?"

Jack shows him his driver's license and they trample over the rocky shore toward where he had left the foot, half buried in the gravel, untouched except from where he had turned it over.

The first constable, whose name tag reads Dee, looks at the shoe on the stony beach. "Did you touch anything?"

Trying to maintain a level of respect, Jack answers, "No, sir, except when I first turned the shoe over with my rod."

"What is your address, sir?"

"I have a cabin on a small island just off Valdes. You can see it from here. There's no street address. I have a PO box at Thetis Island Marina."

"Occupation?"

"Retired."

The constable finally takes a couple of cell phone pictures of the foot before unceremoniously dumping the foot into a plastic bag. The constables take no note of any of the surroundings. No other photos. No care to the area, which is a potential crime scene. It's hard for Jack to discern if incompetence stems from sheer laziness or just a lack of general intelligence. Probably a combination of the two, but whichever, it annoys him.

"Pardon me for asking, but don't you guys want to seal off the scene?"

"What scene, sir? You found a shoe. There's no sign of foul play here."

"I found a shoe with a *foot* inside it. Aren't you the least bit curious about where the rest of him is?"

"*Possible* foot. It could be a hoax just like the one up in Campbell River."

"Well, wouldn't a hoax still be a crime?"

He smiles patronizingly. "You can leave the investigation to us, sir. We'll be in touch if we need anything. Have a good day, eh?"

The constables get back into their boat with the evidence bag, shove off, starting the motor, and roar across the bay in a smooth curve. It's still early in the day, but Jack needs another drink. Dealing with idiots generally makes him feel that way.

5

The next morning, Liz waits patiently for the press conference to start. They are about to announce the capture of the elusive Stanley Park Rapist. Women will be able to sleep better at night knowing he is behind bars. Or at least, that's the hope. Reporters are buzzing in the small media room.

Inspector Michelle Ward, Liz's superior, will introduce her. Ward is career RCMP and a mentor to Liz. She went to bat for Liz when she suggested the honey trap to catch Timmons. Liz, a butterfly bandage over her eye, looking modest and battered in her uniform, waits beside Ward, who steps to the podium.

"Good morning. The RCMP has detained one William Timmons, as a person of interest in the Stanley Park Rapist case. Our very own media liaison officer, Liz MacDonald courageously volunteered for the sting operation. I'm sure you will all portray her in an appropriately heroic light."

Scattered laughter. Liz steps up to the podium, pauses for the buzz to settle down.

"In a joint task force between RCMP and Vancouver PD, after a series of surveillance operations, Mr. Timmons was apprehended and is being charged with battery, resisting arrest and assaulting an officer. Are there any questions?"

Liz nods to one reporter whose hand is raised.

"What about rape? Is he being indicted for the seven rapes that occurred in Stanley Park?"

"As Inspector Ward stated, Mr. Timmons is a person of interest in these attacks. The Crown Attorney is reviewing the case. As it stands, Mr. Timmons is being held for assault and resisting arrest."

"How'd you get that shiner?"

Liz frowns. "Apprehending the suspect."

Another of the reporter pool regulars, an aging beauty with dark hair and eyes, raises her hand. "Rosie George, of the blog Missing-Missing.com."

The pool reacts and despite snickers from the other reporters in the room, Rosie continues, "Is there any connection between the more than forty missing-person cases in the Lower Mainland and the Stanley Park Rapist?"

Liz glances at Inspector Ward. "We ah, no, we . . . have no evidence of any such connection."

Rosie persists, "Forty unsolved missing persons and no ideas, no leads, no connections?"

"Ah, there is no evidence that our suspect is connected to any crimes other than the Stanley Park attacks. We profiled a sexual predator. We established his patterns, we set up a sting operation and were able to apprehend him. And regarding your question, we are giving *all* our missing person cases our fullest attention." She nods to another reporter.

"What about the severed foot discovered yesterday on Valdes Island?"

Liz breathes out, glances at Ward. How had *that* slipped by her?

Ward steps up, says, "It's too early in our investigation to comment on—"

Rosie interrupts. "Really? What about a connection to the severed feet and missing persons? What are we up to now, twelve? Thirteen feet?"

Liz, frustrated, says, "There is no known connection between the Stanley Park Rapist, missing people or the severed feet. Furthermore there is no sign of foul play with regard to the feet. They're not severed. They were naturally disarticulated, probably by decomposition in the sea."

"Really? Are there thirteen healthy people stumbling around with a missing foot who haven't bothered phoning you?" Rosie has scored a point and the reporters laugh. Inspector Ward breaks in.

"Thank you very much ladies and gentlemen, but that's a separate matter. That's all we have time for today. Thank you!"

Rosie gets more agitated. "This is the Pig Farmer Murders all over again! You ignored the truth then and you're ignoring it now!"

"Ma'am, please calm down," says Ward.

"This is a cover-up!"

Two officers try to gently escort Rosie out as she continues to create a ruckus.

"I will not be silenced! Remember the Missing-Missing!"

■ ■ ■

Michelle Ward slams down Timmons' file on her desk.

"Timmons is out."

Liz can't believe it. "What?"

"Vancouver PD wants him out. VPD thinks we bungled the arrest on their turf and they're not going to take the heat. It was supposed to be a joint operation."

"What was joint about it?" asks Liz. "They did nothing to help."

"Beside the point. What's more, the Crown Attorney is 'unwilling to indict him at this time.' It gets worse. Timmons and his lawyer are suing the RCMP for entrapment, police brutality, wrongful arrest and defamation of character. What the hell went wrong here, people?"

Liz wasn't expecting to be on the hot seat.

"As it says in my report, ma'am. He tackled me from behind. We scuffled. He attempted to get zip ties on my wrists and sexually assault me. I broke free. I tried to arrest him. He hit me with a stick and had to be subdued before my backup arrived." Liz glances at Richards and Fouché.

"So you beat *him* with a stick? Tit for tat?"

"I hit him once. I defended myself as best I could, without backup. I wasn't going to get raped by that sonofabitch."

"And where was your backup?"

Richards pauses, clears his throat. "There was some confusion about the right trail. By the time we arrived at the scene, Corporal MacDonald had the situation under control."

"And now you three may have put that 'sonofabitch' back on the street."

Liz looks down. Fouché, as if noticing her struggle, steps in.

"What about DNA? If we link him to the rapes, we can still arrest him."

Ward shakes her head. "The guy is good. He has never left DNA behind. No saliva. No semen. No skin under victims' fingernails."

Liz can't believe they had so little before they sent her into the woods.

"What? How? He has seven victims and counting!"

"The victims were all subdued with zip ties and he used condoms."

"So, we have no hard evidence linking him to the rapes?" Fouché asks.

Liz persists, "This isn't some guy out for a jog. He used a blitz attack. He's a power-assertive rapist. He doesn't have a problem using force, which he did when he hit me and tried to beat me up. Roughing me up just added to his arousal. Isn't there anything we can use?"

"You can't prove a hard-on because he hit you, Liz."

"Thanks Richards. Tell me something I don't know. He tried to zip-tie me and told me I was going to like it. That coincides. Can't we use *that*?"

Ward shakes her head. "Just circumstantial. Nothing that would stick in court."

Richards boils over. "If you hadn't screwed up the sting by slugging this guy, we'd have him."

"Well maybe if you didn't take your sweet time backing me up I wouldn't have had to slug him!"

Ward can see this is going south fast. "This isn't getting us anywhere. Gentlemen. That will be all."

Richards and Fouché leave. Richards glares at Liz as he exits. Ward turns to Liz, motions her to stay.

"Liz, I am going to pull you from the Stanley Park Rapist case."

"I see . . ."

"I know it's a raw deal. But we are in a political mess here. The Vancouver PD is upset that our joint effort blew up. The Crown Attorney is livid. If it were up to me . . ."

"What can I do to make this right? I can be of more value to the RCMP than just Media Liaison. And quite honestly, after yesterday's press conference, we may have a PR storm brewing."

"How so?"

"I did some research on Rosie George. At first blush, she may seem like a nut but she has a large online following. And not just conspiracy theorists. She is acting almost like a victim's advocate. Plus, I think she has a point."

"Which is?"

"The RCMP is seen as inattentive to the missing and disenfranchised. Prostitutes, addicts, runaways. The 'Missing-Missing.'"

"We take all crimes seriously. You know that."

"Between the Highway of Tears up north and the Pickton Murder debacle, people might disagree. It's about the public's perception. Every family of a missing person deserves an answer."

"What are you suggesting?"

"Maybe Rosie is onto something. Maybe there is a link between missing people and the severed feet case, for starters."

"There is no severed feet case."

"Okay. Why not? Those feet belong to *somebody*. If they aren't reported, they have to match some of our missing persons. And if we have feet floating around, where are the bodies?"

"You're right. That's why I'm also putting you on the E-Beacon Missing Persons task force."

Liz is surprised. "Ah, thank you. Who am I working with?"

"Richards and Fouché. Richards is senior so he has the lead. Your Media Liaison duties come first."

Liz can't hide her disappointment.

"They're good investigators Liz. This is an opportunity for the three of you to sort things out. Do you want the assignment or not?"

"Of course. I'll do whatever it takes."

"And as Media Liaison, you know what is at stake here. We don't want to create widespread panic."

"Inspector Ward, with all due respect, we have been hypersensitive about the matter regarding the severed feet since the Vancouver Olympics. We can't rule out all foul play possibilities simply because we have an aversion to bad publicity."

"Let's start with the least romantic scenarios like plane crashes, industrial accidents and suicides before we jump to serial killers, okay?"

"Of course. But if those options are eliminated, we go where the investigation takes us. Right?"

"Liz, as far as the public is concerned, regarding feet—there is no Bigfoot, no aliens, and there is definitely and under no circumstances a serial killer. Are we clear?"

6

Mist rises from the harbor as Liz sets off on her usual morning run along the seawall. She is barely visible through the fog. Some mornings are harder than others but she finally gets a steady rhythm going. The morning aches and pains work their way through her body.

Her mind wanders as she runs. *My shin splints are acting up. Am I due for a new pair of running shoes? How many miles have I put on with this pair? Why are feet washing ashore in running shoes? Only running shoes? Because shoes float? Are they only runners who are missing feet? What kind of break can I make in this case? I need to get a whiteboard. That will help. If things calm down, should I get a dog? Running with a dog would be nice. Maybe safer. Maybe a shepherd-Lab mix just like old Black Jack. He was such a sweet boy.*

Then, like a flash of light, a sudden image of a man's hand raised with a belt invades her stream of consciousness. The harsh snap and the pain.

Liz picks up her pace. She doesn't want to think about that. But she does. Like telling someone not to think about an elephant. She shivers as she remembers the belt snapping down again with a wicked slap. And again. The searing pain. The helplessness. The betrayal. The shocking fear like a mouthful of copper pennies.

Liz speeds up again. Maybe a sprint will refocus her. She turns into the forest past first-growth cedars, over the footbridge, speeds up her pace. She hesitates at the side trail where she first met Timmons—ominous with mist and shadows—she bypasses it and continues down the trail to the seawall. Does she hear footsteps? She runs faster. She ducks behind a tree and turns to look. No one is there. She feels silly. Shakes it off and continues running. A nice jog along the seawall, into the pale sunshine.

■ ■ ■

Armed with coffee, two fried egg sandwiches, an egg white omelet and a wheatgrass shooter, Liz enters the conference room, nervous about her first meeting with Richards and Fouché. The room is littered with stacks of file boxes. There is a clean whiteboard on the wall with "E-Beacon Task Force" written along the top. The two men look up from their coffee.

"Morning, guys. I brought breakfast."

Fouché looks at the to-go bag. "Thanks, but I don't eat fast food."

"I know. That's why I brought you something horribly green and an egg white omelet."

"Oh. How'd you know?"

"Just a hunch. And for Richards and I, something wonderfully greasy and delicious."

Richards laughs. "You hit it on the head with the breakfast. Let's see how far your deductive reasoning takes you on Missing Persons."

Liz sits down. Richards takes a large bite of his sandwich before he speaks.

"Inspector Ward believes we can work together despite yesterday's incident. I feel the same way. If anyone has a problem, I want to know now."

Liz nods, takes a moment, treads lightly. "No problem, except I need to know if you guys have my back."

"We do. But there's more to it than that."

"I don't follow."

"One day, you are going to be alone, no backup coming with a perp who outweighs you by forty kilos. How will you handle it?"

"You mean like yesterday? Ask Timmons how it worked out." So much for treading lightly. "So, now that you know how I will 'handle a bad guy' all by myself, I need to know from here on out: do you have my back?"

"Of course we do," says Richards. "All right, then. We have over seven thousand missing people in BC and thirteen severed feet. I think we should start with the medical examiner."

■ ■ ■

The Gulf Islands, a string of elongated, timbered islands scattered along the southeast shore of Vancouver Island, are a vacation spot for thousands, a home for a few. It's an escape that you can only get to by boat, ferry or floatplane. Not many people live on the islands in the fall or winter, which is fine with Jack Harris, who doesn't really like company anyway.

A steady rain drips from the conifers, making a soothing sound on Jack's roof. A dilapidated, thirty-two-foot, wooden sailboat, *Skookum*, low in the water and listing to starboard, is tied up to Jack's dock. The dock is strewn with various small boats island-dwellers collect, like a sea kayak and a leaky, aluminum speedboat with a cracked windshield and a rain canopy, known as a "tinner". Jack's cabin is a simple, tiny L-shaped summer cottage, without central heating, built just above high-water mark. A lantern within reflects through the dusk onto the dark water below. The interior is sparsely decorated, with one striking BC native carving, a parting gift from his ex-wife. There is a menagerie of fly-fishing equipment and outdoor sporting gear scattered on shelves and tables throughout the cabin. An ancient threadbare recliner has the place of honor near a cozy fire in his woodstove, courtesy of Jack's labor. Who needs a gym when there is a cord of wood to split and stack? A perfect setup, except the one problem with living in a summer home is that it is designed for summer, not fall or winter. Consequently, there's a constant, damp chill throughout the cabin. Nothing a good fire and a stiff drink can't dispel, however.

Jack is seated at his kitchen table doing some preliminary online research on the severed feet mystery, armed with his laptop and drink, which he is just refreshing. On his screen, Jack pulls up headline after headline, and several videos of news reports about the twelve severed feet that have washed up on the shores and islands. His foot is number thirteen. He clicks on several YouTube news videos:

> *"Four human feet have washed up along the shores of the Pacific Northwest."*
> *"Scientists speculate feet are remains from Asian tsunami."*
> *"Is it sinister?"*
> *"The thing is, it's not the first time, not the second or even the third time that this has happened— "*
> *"Another foot washes up on the south coast. This one in Richmond. The seventh since last August."*
> *"Tenth foot found in False Creek."*
> *"Did Bigfoot attack?"*

Jack pours himself another drink and then prints out several articles on the same themes.

He thinks, *Well, these feet can't be good for the vacation business.*

■ ■ ■

Liz strolls into the medical examiner's examination room with Richards and Fouché. The room is filled with body drawers and metal tables under harsh fluorescent lights. The inescapable ammonia reek of formalin and death – a metallic mix of must and old blood. The room is excessively cold, like walking into a refrigerator.

The medical examiner, Zach Kallan, is young but his talent belies his age. He pulls a foot out of a cooler drawer. His gruesome artifact is in an advanced state of decay, bones and long nails protruding through rotted flesh. The shoe is on a tray behind it. Richards pulls back and covers his nose with his sleeve.

"What can you tell us?"

"Right human foot found by a local on Valdes Island. Women's size 7 Reebok manufactured in Canada in 2008. DNA is viable but we have nothing to match it to."

Liz looks at the foot. "How long was it in the water?"

"Hard to say. The shoe protects the foot, so I can't determine how long it's been submerged."

She says, "What are the similarities to the other feet?"

"All were in running shoes. Most likely because the buoyancy of the shoe allows it to float."

Fouché asks, "Male or female?"

"Based on the shoes, probably female."

Zach turns to a drawer and pulls out a few of the other feet and shoes in plastic bags. Zach delicately pulls one of the feet out of its bag. A putrid smell, like rotting chicken, wafts inescapably into the air. Liz reacts, involuntarily covering her mouth and nose.

"This foot was found in the Fraser River. It is a woman's left foot. The shoe was a size 8 Nike; made in 2010."

Richards checks his notebook. "Naturally disarticulated, right?"

"As far as I can tell. No striations on the bone from a tool or saw."

Liz won't accept the obvious answer. "Could striations have been smoothed down by wave action, kind of like sea glass? Or could it have been an amputation with a surgeon's scalpel cutting between the bones?"

"Conceivably . . ."

"So we can't definitively say if it was or wasn't foul play?"

"Pretty hard without a body."

"We need to match a body to a foot," says Fouché.

Richards closes his notebook. "That's one fucked-up Cinderella story."

He turns to Liz and Fouché. "We need a list of high-probability people missing since 2006, women, runners between the ages of sixteen and forty."

Liz nods. "And we need to go the families for DNA. We should cross-reference cold cases, mutilation murders and the shoes' manufacturer dates. Let's see if we get lucky."

Richards says wryly, "Better lucky than good. See what you both can come up with."

■ ■ ■

The rain has stopped. Drips off the eaves patter as Jack continues his online research. It's amazing what you can find on YouTube. All on one website you can find clips ranging from "I Love Lucy" to news reports of severed feet. His favorite so far was from *The Rachel Maddow Show* where she quips to the camera, "Yeah, wow, I can't believe we're talking nine feet . . . Nine!"

We're up to thirteen, what do you think now, Rachel? Jack wonders. Another such video features Liz MacDonald, the acting RCMP spokesperson with delightfully unkempt hair. She's a looker; he'll give her that. Pretty typical for PR gals. Best to deliver bad news with a pretty face.

He presses play. Liz speaks at an earlier press conference: "Much of the discussion involves the feet being severed. There is no evidence that these feet have been severed. I will note that these are very challenging samples. Being in the water is the worst-case scenario for DNA recovery. But to reiterate, there is no evidence that the feet have been forcibly removed."

Jack pulls up a freeze-frame of Liz on screen. He takes a screen grab and prints out her picture, then steps back and looks at his detective's "Wall of Infamy." To the normal person it's a gruesome collage. To a former detective, these

pictures of feet, articles and maps with pins showing locations of where feet have been found may spark some kind
of link or association. Beside his collage is a whiteboard
with bullet points about the case scribbled on it. He adds
Liz's picture to the wall.

7

Liz is home alone in her austere East Van ground-floor apartment. Her only furniture of note is a treadmill. It's not that she dislikes decorating or lacks the money to do so; it is just too much of a hassle. The time it takes to shop and pick it out, to clean the extra stuff. And Ikea makes her gag. No thanks. Streamlined is just fine.

The glow from her laptop lights up her face as she reads from Rosie George's blog, TheMissing-Missing.com:

> *I just left the press conference at the RCMP. If you can even call it that. Liz MacDonald, media puppet, I mean liaison, looking like Royal Canadian Mountie Barbie, stepped heroically up to the podium to give her usual spiel of nonsense we have grown accustomed to from RCMP. "There is no sign of foul play" . . . "There is no connection between the Stanley Park*

Rapist and the feet." . . . *"There is no connection between the feet and missing persons."* . . . *"The feet have not actually been severed. Just dismembered." Explain the difference to me, Mountie Barbie.*

Well, the last time I checked, I haven't heard of thirteen people hopping around on one foot in the Lower Mainland. Those bodies have to be somewhere and those people have to be missing. I know there are those out there who don't want to hear what I have to say. What does Rosie George know? She is just some junkie hooker . . . Well, I know this: the RCMP doesn't investigate crimes against the disenfranchised as actively crimes against affluent whites. Don't believe me? Ask the forty-some-odd First Nations families whose daughters disappeared on the Highway of Tears up north, near Hazelton. They don't give drug addicts or prostitutes a fair shake either. They chose a "dangerous lifestyle" so they deserve what they get. Well guess what? Not everyone has the same choices in life. I didn't. I know how the streets work. I know that when street girls go missing, their families have no idea because they were already missing. No one misses the Missing-Missing. But I do. And I will find out what happened to them even if RCMP won't.

Liz blows a stray hair from her eyes as she prints out the article. As her mother used to say, you have to take the bad with the good. She looks at it and then tapes it to her wall, which now includes a map, more articles and pictures of the feet. One half is labeled *Severed Feet.* The other *Stanley Park Rapes.*

Liz gets up and heads to the window and looks outside as if searching for something. No inspiration or answers to her questions there, she shuts her window and pulls the blind. Her phone rings. Startled, she jumps, and then answers it.

"Liz MacDonald."

"Liz? It's Doug."

"Hi. What's up?"

"Look, I just wanted to apologize personally for what happened the other day. Richards is kind of old-school and I shouldn't have gone along with it but I did. I was kind of between a rock and a hard place. He's my superior but I knew he was wrong. I just want you to know I take responsibility for that."

"Thanks. Yeah, I get it. Okay. Let's move on. Actually, I'm glad you called. I was looking at the most recent severed foot report and it's pretty incomplete. I think we should interview the guy who found it."

She consults her notepad. "One Jack Harris, lives in a cabin on some island near Valdes."

"Sure, we can go out tomorrow morning. I'll clear it with Richards. This time, I'll pick up breakfast."

■ ■ ■

Morning. Jack, slightly hung-over and well into a morning six-pack of beer, is working on the in-board engine on *Skookum*, his ancient sailboat. At least he was until he passed out on the settee.

A shadow floats past the dusty porthole outside, foot-steps, and the boat rocks slightly as someone steps aboard. The movement wakes Jack, who sees the shadow through the porthole. His survival mode kicks in. In one smooth motion, he grabs a large boat knife and steps behind the cabin door as a man dressed in a Barbour jacket steps warily into the boat's cabin, backlit in the companionway.

Without hesitation, Jack jumps him and expertly flips him onto the deck. Suddenly a pistol is cocked behind Jack's right ear.

"RCMP! Freeze! Drop the knife!"

Liz, at the top of the ladder, has got the drop on Jack. Jack drops his boat knife. Fouché, on the floor, stunned and winded, gets up furious and picks up the knife.

"Thanks, Liz."

"Don't mention it."

Fouché roughly knocks Jack's knees out from under him, searches him and tightly cuffs him facedown on the deck.

"You are under arrest. You have the right to retain counsel. You have the right—"

"Take it easy! I'm a cop! Check my wallet."

"Really? Why were you resisting arrest?"

"What are you arresting me for?"

"Resisting arrest."

"For Christ sake you never ID'd yourselves. All I saw was a stranger entering my boat."

Liz helps Jack up. "Let's go up to your cabin and have a chat."

On the dock, Liz leads Jack past an RCMP Zodiac with two constables waiting in it. They stand but Liz waves them off. Jack recognizes them from the other day.

"Give my regards to Tweedle Dee and Tweedle Dum."

"You know them?"

"Yeah, they came to collect the foot I found. Top-notch police work."

They get to Jack's cabin door and look to Jack, who shrugs.

"There's no lock. I'd open the door for you but . . ."

"That's okay, I've got it."

The three enter. Jack sits down at his kitchen table, still cuffed. Liz takes a look at his Wall of Infamy and the empty bottles of Macallan, and then turns to Jack.

"We'd like to question you about the foot you found."

"Then take off the cuffs."

"Not so fast, you assaulted an officer."

"I assaulted a trespasser. Aren't you Corporal MacDonald, the RCMP's media gal?"

"Yes. I am also on the E-Beacon Missing Person's task force. This is Corporal Doug Fouché."

Jack nods to him. "Pleasure. Are you a media gal, too?"

"The pleasure is all mine." Fouché points to Jack's wall. "You seem to have an unhealthy interest in severed feet."

"You would too if you found one."

"Your wall looks a lot like a serial killer's 'I love me' wall."

"Or an analysis wall for an investigation, which you folks don't seem too interested in. Are you going to tell me my foot is probably from some tsunami victim or an unreported plane crash?"

Liz tries to defuse. "We will need to examine the evidence before we make any conclusions, sir."

"Spoken just like a media gal."

Liz scans Jack's cabin. Jack's memorabilia of twenty-five years on the Force in Seattle adorns the wall—a framed photo of him accepting an award from Seattle's mayor, a plaque for Officer of the Year commending his dedicated and loyal service.

"You're a detective with Seattle PD?"

"Was. I'm retired."

"You're pretty young to retire."

"Thank you. I got tired of being a cop."

Fouché looks around. "Do you have any firearms?"

"A shotgun. Licensed and locked up."

"What do you need a shotgun for Mr. Harris?"

"Ducks."

Fouché smiles. "They *are* dangerous this time of year. We're going to need that gun, sir."

"Why? There isn't buckshot in the foot."

Liz steps in. "How do you know that, Mr. Harris?"

Fouché adds, "I think we better continue this chat downtown."

"There's an original line. Am I under arrest?"

Liz hesitates, unlocks Jack's handcuffs. Fouché gives her a look.

"No. Your cooperation is voluntary and would be greatly appreciated."

Jack rubs his wrists. "Whatever I can do to be of service."

Fouché points to Jack's feet photos. "Let's take his 'I love me' wall with us while we're at it."

8

Jack is used to sitting on the other side of the table in an interrogation room but it can cut both ways. He has nothing to hide and based on his research, the RCMP does.

He sits with his arms crossed, waiting for their approach.

Liz and Fouché sit opposite Jack. Liz looks at her notes while Fouché idly flips through the photos from Jack's wall.

"Tell us everything about the foot you found."

"It was a foot, in a running shoe, on the beach."

"Anything else?"

"I told the constables everything. Check their notes."

"Can you just walk us through it?"

"I was fishing for sea-run cutthroat yesterday around 6:45 AM. It was high tide. I was using a number 6 muddler minnow. Caught a nice one, at least eighteen inches. A beauty."

Liz is not amused. "More about the foot, please."

Jack shrugs. "I guess you're not a fisherman. I saw this shoe. I turned it over with the bottom of my rod. There was what appeared to be a decayed foot inside. I called it in."

Fouché steps in. "Did you leave the shoe at any time?"

"No. Wouldn't want it to walk away."

"Is there anyone else on the island to verify your story?"

"I live on a summer island in the *winter*. What do you think?"

Fouché slaps the file on the table. "I think it's suspicious that you collect photos of severed feet, Mr. Harris. How long have you been in Canada?"

"Since last year."

"Are you a permanent resident?"

"I plan to be. I filed my landed immigrant paperwork last month."

"We'll see about that."

"You do that. Am I a suspect?"

"You are now. You claim to have found a severed foot and you used a knife to attack an officer of the law."

"Good for you. I was beginning to believe you didn't think there was a crime involved."

Liz can tell Jack is taking over the session and it annoys her. "There isn't."

"Because you don't have a body? Why haven't you used cadaver dogs? Or better yet, gall wasps? Have you even secured the area? Right now, you should be checking my cabin for a basement or an attic, tearing my place apart looking for hair, fibers, blood—anything linking me to a crime. Are you doing any of that? Why haven't you been investigating this as a crime? Does the RCMP just brush everything under the rug? Evil only permeates the United States? Canada is immune to serial killers?"

Liz and Fouché share a look.

Fouché responds, "Just let us ask the questions, Mr. Harris."

"Funny, that's what your constables said."

Jack looks at both investigators. Could they really be this naïve or were they just towing the company line? He decides to find out.

"You're not going to find him."

"Excuse me?" says Fouché.

"You're not going find him. He lives among you, but you won't find him." He waits for it to land. "Because you don't want to."

"Are you saying RCMP doesn't want to find serial killers?" Fouché looks hard at Jack.

"No. I'm saying no one wants to find *this* one. He's not just evil, he is evil incarnate. Better that he live just outside the pale of consciousness, in the darkness, than be captured, brought to light like a chained beast in broad daylight. You won't bring this one in. If you do, you'll wish you hadn't."

Liz interjects, "You're wrong. We will find him. And he will receive justice."

"You don't understand. This one's different. Most serial killers want to get caught. He *doesn't*. He doesn't leave clues to show how clever he is. He's not leaving a breadcrumb trail to his house in the woods."

Liz looks at him. *Is this guy for real?*

"Thanks for that cheery assessment."

Jack shrugs. "I'm here to help."

Liz nods to Fouché and they step outside the interrogation room.

■ ■ ■

Michelle Ward and Richards have been watching the interview from the other side of the glass. Liz and Fouché exit the interview room to confer with them. It's not often they interrogate another cop. Or former cop, if his story holds water.

Fouché says, "That took a creepy turn. I don't like him."

Richards replies, "We have nothing to hold him on. And he's not really a suspect."

"What about the shotgun?"

Ward hands a file to Fouché.

"It's legal. He checks out. I spoke to his former commanding officer in Seattle. Said Jack Harris was their top expert on serial killers. He's the guy who shot the Bellevue Butcher. Took 'early retirement.'"

"You mean he is *the* Jack Harris?" says Fouché. "I heard that wasn't exactly a clean shoot."

"He's one of the good guys."

"Cops don't ever murder people?"

Ward stands firm. "Cut him loose. But keep an eye on him. We don't need him playing Dirty Harry in our backyard."

Liz and Fouché step back into the interrogation room.

"Mr. Harris. You're free to go, sorry for any confusion. And if you have any other information, please call me." Liz hands him her card.

Jack takes her card. "I always enjoy consulting with my colleagues."

He grabs his coat. Liz hands Jack back his feet file. He hesitates at the door.

"Isn't this where you say, 'We'll be in touch, Mr. Harris'?"

Liz smiles. "Thank you for your cooperation, Mr. Harris."

9

Jack is walking down Georgia Street, near the RCMP head-quarters, looking in vain for a cab. It's been a long afternoon and he wants to get home. His right hand has developed a noticeable tremor. He looks down at it, balls it into a fist and shoves the fist into his jeans pocket. He passes a bar with an all-glass front. He pauses.

The bar is sleek, modern—ferns, stainless steel and blond wood. Not his usual style, but then again as long as they serve whiskey, anything is his style. Jack turns back and goes inside. He sits at the bar near the window and looks at the liquors lit up enticingly behind the bartender. The television is playing the six o'clock local news while various patrons are watching it or immersed in their private conversations. The comforting familiarity and mutual ano-nymity of the saloon.

Jack listens to the newscaster: "Foot number thirteen has washed ashore. This time on Valdes Island. RCMP spokesperson Liz MacDonald stated no foul play is suspected."

Jack looks up at the TV just as the bartender switches the channel from Liz's face to the hockey game.

The bartender is annoyed. "Such rubbish. Thirteen feet, how dumb do they think we are?"

One of his regulars looks at him. "Pretty dumb! Everyone knows it's Bigfoot!"

"I don't know about that one, Woody. Bigfoot is a gentle spirit." The bartender notices Jack. "What can I getcha?"

"The Macallan… Make it a double."

The bartender delivers the drink. Jack downs it. The long, smooth burn.

Jack points to his glass. "Again, please."

"Rough day?"

"Nothing Dr. Macallan can't fix."

The bartender pours another single malt and slides it to Jack. Jack takes another drink. His hand stops shaking. As he nurses the rest of his drink, he puts his back to the bar and watches people passing by the window. Liz MacDonald rushes past in uniform, briefcase, eco-to-go coffee cup in hand. Jack hesitates, puts down his drink and goes outside. He hurries to catch up with her.

Jack calls after Liz, "You're quite the celebrity, Corporal MacDonald."

Liz puts her hand in her shoulder bag as she turns around.

"Hi. Sorry." Raising his hands. "Don't shoot."

"This is Canada. We're not armed off-duty. I'm heading home right now, why don't you call me tomorrow?" She takes her hand off the pepper spray inside her purse.

"Can I buy you a drink?"

Liz looks Jack over. "I'm still in uniform."

"I'm sure they'd have a latte or something."

She shows him her cup. "Thanks, Mr. Harris but I'm good."

"OK, can I buy myself one and you can watch me drink it?"

"Looks like you already had a couple."

"I think we got off on the wrong foot."

"Very funny."

"I want to apologize for not being very helpful. Please, just ten minutes."

Liz blows the air out between her cheeks and follows Jack inside.

■ ■ ■

In a booth, Jack takes another drink while Liz nurses her coffee. Jack looks at her. She seems reasonable. Maybe. He pulls out pictures from his file.

"Two feet is an anomaly, three to four feet is statistically curious, five to six feet, you have to think dirty. But *thirteen feet*? And 'no sign of foul play'? *Seriously*?"

"This isn't Seattle."

"No it's BC—World Capitol of Missing Persons. You've got 7,200 of 'em. And you're not investigating this as a crime?"

"British Columbia has over 4.6 million people. That's not really statistically relevant."

"Tell that to the families."

"No need to be snide, Mr. Harris."

"Call me Jack."

"No need to be snide, Jack. Look, we are investigating. I saw the foot myself. There are no tool marks on the ankle-bones. No saws, no discernible knife marks. There are no signs of foul play and nothing to link the feet to—"

"Really? What about the footless body that washed up on Orcas Island in 2007?"

Liz hesitates. "That was on the US side."

"So what? They haven't solved that one either. Orcas Island is only twenty miles from here and ten miles from Valdes. You have to think outside the box. A murderer could have weighed down the bodies, dumped them in the water and the feet came off some time after. The currents could carry them for miles."

"There are a variety of possibilities other than murder."

"Like Bigfoot?"

Liz is undeterred. "Industrial, boating accidents, tug-boat accidents, car wrecks, suicides . . ."

"Let me stop you right here. In crime, there is no such thing as coincidence."

"Is that official Seattle PD doctrine?"

"No, it's Sherlock Holmes. What you have here is a serial killer. And your foot guy, he is a psychopath, not a sociopath."

"Why is that significant?"

Jack begins his rapid-fire. "Because sociopaths are more erratic and impulsive. Not psychopaths. Your guy has no autonomic arousal, so emotions won't affect his endgame. He is meticulous. He has above-average intelligence, blends in with society, and has a regular life that masks his secret one."

"Ah, okay. But why feet?"

"It's a ritual. He is process-focused and the mutilation is probably more important than the killing itself. Dismemberment also has a sexual component. Think Ed Gein, Jeffrey Dahmer. Maybe he has been mutilated or injured in some way and he's acting out his rage."

"Anything else?"

"He likes making the RCMP look like fools." Jack raises his glass.

Liz looks at him wryly. "Just like you?"

■ ■ ■

Richards and Fouché enter and sidle up to the bar. It's been a long day. Richards has invited Fouché for a drink after their shift. Normally Fouché doesn't drink but sometimes you have to be one of the guys if you want to get ahead. Richards spots Liz with Jack, seated in the back.

Richards nudges Fouché. "That's awfully cozy, don't you think?"

"Maybe she's trying to use her feminine charms to get some answers."

"I thought she didn't like him for this."

"I didn't think she did."

"Maybe she just likes him."

Fouché looks at Liz and Jack.

"Please. He's too old for her."

"Shit, I'd bang her if I had the chance."

"Like that would happen."

"Wait a second." Richards grins. "You have a hard-on for her."

"She's not my type. And I don't date colleagues."

"She's anybody's type. Faint heart never fucked fair maiden." Richards gets the bartender's attention.

"Bartender, I'll take a beer and get my friend here something with an umbrella."

■ ■ ■

Jack pulls his map out of his file. Puts the map, detailing where the feet have been found, down in front of Liz.

"Okay, so why no floating feet before 2007? We've had running shoes since the seventies and never had feet floating ashore before."

"Maybe there were and they went unnoticed."

"And maybe there's a Santa Claus." Jack finishes his last slug of Scotch. "Well, I've got to catch the ferry."

"Okay. Thanks."

He shakes her hand, starts off. She calls after him.

"Mr. Harris . . ." Liz smiles at him. "We'll be in touch."

Richards and Fouché take all of this in. They turn away as Jack walks past. Richards watches Jack out of the corner of his eye as he passes the window.

"I'm not sure about that one. We'll have to keep an eye on him."

■ ■ ■

In the last of the summer twilight, Jack stands on the bow of the ferry winding into the labyrinth of the Gulf Islands, brooding, leaning on the rail, staring into the cold, thickening wind and gathering gloom as the sun sets behind Vancouver Island. Some people find taking a ferry to get to your home inconvenient, and if you are in a hurry, it is, but Jack doesn't have much need to be in a hurry these days. Not since he retired. It was just a matter of time, he guessed. He was never known as a "team player". He didn't get along with his new commanding officer and despite Jack's track record for being able to track down the toughest killers, the commander ran out of patience for Jack's unorthodox behavior based on "hunches and alcoholic intuition."

Granted, Jack's drinking *had* gotten heavier over time but for God's sake, *something* was needed to numb the constant visions of the horror his job entailed. The last guy. He was evil. He targeted teen runaways, which there were plenty of in the outskirts of Seattle. Some kicked out and discarded by their families like yesterday's trash. It was easier for a stray dog to get shelter than a teen runaway.

The killer would prowl the Pioneer Square scene, stalking girls on the game, looking for dates. The thing about runaways, no one would notice if they were missing. It could take weeks or months before they were on anyone's radar. But they were on Jack's radar after his friend Julia, who worked at a teen shelter, came to him when one of her favorite clients didn't show up.

Julia told him about Peanut. A five-foot-nothing, wisp of a girl. Peanut never missed the weekly Ping-Pong tournament they held every Thursday. You didn't have to be big to be good at Ping-Pong and Peanut loved it.

Jack surmised that maybe Peanut got a good score and was in a drug den somewhere. But Julia was insistent. She had boots on the ground and no one had seen or heard from Peanut in days. And there was more: other girls had been disappearing. As a courtesy, Jack looked into it, and his friend was right. Fifteen girls had disappeared over the course of six months. All within a two-mile perimeter of Pioneer Square. It seemed too coincidental.

After months of investigating, Jack knew he had a serial killer on his hands. The bastard was luring hookers, drug addicts and street kids, then taking them to his house in Bellevue, where he literally butchered them like cattle. This guy had a fixation with Jack the Ripper, even left taunting "catch me if you can" notes. Jack narrowed down his search to several johns who frequented the area. He got a handwriting match through public documents to determine which was his prime suspect but couldn't gather enough hard evidence for an arrest warrant.

One night, after staking him out, Jack followed the killer into the back streets of Seattle. The guy was about to lure a girl into his car. She couldn't have been more than fourteen. Jack stopped him but the killer took off in the van. Jack gave chase and cornered him. The guy got out of the van with something in his hand. A gun? Maybe. Probably. Jack wasn't going to wait and find out. He shot the man three times center mass with his 9 mm Glock. He was dead before he hit the ground. Turned out there was no gun and Jack had alcohol in his bloodstream. Jack's commander didn't think it was funny when Jack said, "How drunk could I have been? I hit him three times, center mass." It was stupidity on his part, but he had no regrets about shooting the guy. Jack knew he'd saved that girl from certain gruesome death. It didn't matter if it was quit or get fired, it was time for Jack to go fishing.

■ ■ ■

Liz likes the solitude of night. The quiet and the calm. It gives her time to think and brainstorm. She sits at her kitchen table poring over her research. A half-eaten frozen dinner sits on the table next to a picture of a half-rotted, severed human foot. On her laptop, she clicks on Rosie's blog TheMissing-Missing.com:

Let's do the math, shall we? 1 Stanley Park Rapist attacking blond runners. 13 Severed feet in running shoes. 7200 Missing persons. Am I missing something here or is this not all connected in some way? I guess it's not if the Crown Attorney isn't willing to prosecute a rapist. No one takes missing person cases seriously and the RCMP won't even admit there is a crime with the feet. They want us to believe they all happen to be suicides or some untoward boating or industrial accident. Nice try. It is not a large leap in logic here. This blogger, Rosie George, is going to ask the tough questions until somebody gets some answers.

Liz stands up and steps back to look at her whiteboard. Under the heading PEOPLE WHO HAVE FOUND FEET, Jack's name is at the top along with twelve others. One couple found a foot, out for a morning walk with their little girl. Another woman, looking for sea glass on the rocky shores. Finding a shoe with a foot in it must be quite a surprise to a civilian. She imagines it probably didn't faze Jack. He's seen worse.

She looks over her bullet points under SEVERED FEET: Dismemberment, Sexual component, Feet, Running shoes. PROFILE: Single, White, 30s, Callous, Charming, Controlled, Organized, Psychopath.

Liz steps back and looks over her whiteboard for the Stanley Park Rapist. RAPE VICTIMS: Single young women, Blond, Sexually active, Runners, Running trails. PROFILE: Single, White, 30s, Power-assertive rapist.

She thinks back to the interview with Timmons. He was controlled yet charming. She writes that on his profile and then moves his picture from the Stanley Park Rapist wall to the Severed Feet board. He may be free for now, but she'll get him.

10

The meeting had been set for 9:00 AM, Ward's office, to go over their progress with missing persons.

Ward looks to her team. "So. Where are we?"

Liz looks at Richards. "May I?"

Richards nods. "Be my guest."

"I think there could be a connection between the Stanley Park Rapist and the feet." Liz knows it is a long shot but she has to bring her theory to Ward and Richards. There follows a brief moment of silence.

"I seem to recall telling you to stay away from Timmons," says Ward finally.

"I thought you said stay away from Bigfoot."

"Not funny."

Richards pipes in, "It's a little bit funny. Let's hear her out."

Liz ticks off her points on her fingers. "Timmons goes after runners. All of the severed feet are in running shoes. Timmons is a rapist. Dismemberment has a sexual component. Look at Jeffrey Dahmer."

Richards says, "There is no viable proof that Timmons has raped, let alone murdered, anyone."

"We *believe* he raped," counters Liz. "We just can't send it to trial. It all fits the serial-killer profile. Deep-seated hatred of women. Timmons works as a dog catcher. Is that a sanctioned way of mistreating animals?"

"That's a stretch."

"Not at all. Animal cruelty is a common precursor to violent sociopathic behavior." Liz continues, "Timmons is a loner, white male in his thirties . . . Former military, served in combat in Afghanistan—possible PTSD could be triggering and escalating the attacks?"

Ward stops Liz. "I think this is still a big jump in logic. PTSD doesn't usually lead to homicide."

"Agreed. But, what if the evidence leads to Timmons?"

"It won't. More importantly, Liz, I hope this kind of tunnel vision doesn't bias your thinking and make you overlook other lines of investigation."

"It won't."

■ ■ ■

Liz dumps her files on her desk. Fouché looks up from his own files and follows her into the conference room.

"Ward is on your case, eh?"

"No more than usual."

Fouché smiles, waves two tickets in front of Liz, conjuring them out of the air like a magician.

"I have tickets on the glass this weekend. Canucks versus Canadiens. Would that cheer you up?"

"Thanks, but I don't date people I work with."

"Me neither. It's not a date. It's hockey!"

Liz smiles. "Tempting. I'd love to see the Canucks beat your Habs, Frenchy."

"Oh? How many cups do the Canucks have? Let me check. Zero? We have—what? Twenty-four? I lose track."

"Ha! That was then, this is now."

Richards walks into the conference room, catching the tail end of their conversation.

"Hey Liz. Know why Canadians do it doggy-style?"

Liz doesn't skip a beat. "So they can both watch the hockey game. And by the way, there is more than *one* way to watch the game, old man."

Fouché laughs. Liz grabs the tickets.

"But the best way is at center ice!"

■ ■ ■

Two bodies slam into the boards right in front of Liz and Fouché, an explosion of ice chips, testosterone and sweat. The glass rattles. They are indeed seated at center ice, right on the glass, dressed in their respective team's jerseys. The crowd in Rogers Arena is electric and the air just crisp enough to let them know they are near the ice. Liz and Fouché go nuts cheering, arguing over the penalty call as the hockey game continues.

Fouché yells, "Boarding!"

"That absolutely was not boarding. Clean hit."

"Please, that was a home ice call. He's such a head-hunter."

"Look Frenchy, diving is for the Olympics . . . unless you're a Hab, then it's just an every-game tactic."

"You're lucky you're a girl, because any other guy I'd have to punch."

"Don't get mad, get even. Winner buys beer."

"Doesn't the loser usually buy?"

"Yeah, but you bought the tickets. So I'd hate for you to have to buy everything."

"That's assuming Habs lose."

"Exactly."

■ ■ ■

After the game, they stop for a quick beer at a sports bar in Yaletown. Liz makes good on her promise and buys the beer for the two of them. Her choice is a strong, hoppy IPA. Liz toasts him. "Ah, the sweet taste of a good win."

Fouché sips his beer, smiles. "This beer is a little bitter."

"No. That would be you after my Canucks trounced your Habs."

"3-2 is hardly a trouncing."

"Ah, we take our small victories where we can, not having the history the Canadiens do."

"You're one of a kind, Liz."

"That I am."

■ ■ ■

They finish their beer and Fouché drives Liz home. It's late. He pulls in and parks his car in front of Liz's duplex. He turns the engine off. There is an uncomfortable pause. Neither knows where this is about to go. Liz grabs her purse and turns to Doug.

"Is this the awkward moment when you try and kiss me?"

Fouché smiles at her. "It would be if this were a date. This was hockey."

"Thanks, Doug. That was really great . . . Good night."

She gets out of the car, turns, knocks on the window. Fouché lowers his window. Is she about to turn this into a date?

She hesitates. "Ah, sorry. I was just wondering . . ."

"Yes, Liz?"

"Want to go for a run tomorrow?"

Fouché thinks about it. "No way, you'd run me into the ground."

"Suit yourself. Go, Canucks, go!!" Liz chants.

Fouché shakes his head, raises his window and drives away. Liz smiles as she heads into her duplex.

■ ■ ■

A bonfire is billowing in the darkness on a secluded beach south of Vancouver, throwing shadows onto the dark, calm water, leaping into the darker forest behind the shore. Music is popping on a stereo. A dozen young friends sharing beer, wine, pot. College kids enjoying a clear fall night before it starts to get too cold. One girl, Amanda, leans against her fiancé, Caleb. She is sun-kissed after the day at the beach, blond hair with highlights bleached from the sun. She shows off her new engagement ring. Her girlfriend grabs her hand and gushes.

"Congratulations! It is lovely!"

"Thank you! I love it."

"Caleb has good taste."

"He certainly does. He's marrying me, right?"

Caleb interjects, "I am right here, you know."

Amanda takes a selfie of her and Caleb. She looks at the time on her phone.

"Uh, oh, it's starting to get late. Come on babe, we have to go. I have cross-country in the morning."

"Let's stay a bit longer."

She kisses him.

"I can't but you can if you want."

"This is why I'm marrying you!"

Amanda grabs her bag, kisses Caleb, and heads to her car.

"Goodnight, my love."

She heads up the narrow path through the trees to her battered Toyota SUV, which is parked underneath a tree on an old logging road with several other cars. Luckily, she has a mini Maglite on her keychain so she can see. Amanda shines the light, clicks her key fob and unlocks the door. She gets in, shuts the door, pulls out her phone and posts a couple of pictures from the party onto Facebook. She starts her engine. A knock on her window. She jumps, looks up, startled, at a man in a hoodie. She rolls down the window. She doesn't know what to say, really.

"Oh . . . Ah . . . Hi."

"Amanda."

The tranquilizer dart hits her neck with a solid *thunk*. It feels like a bee sting. Shocked, she pulls it out of her neck, looks at it incredulously and drops it as she collapses. The man in the hoodie drags her out of the SUV, into the forest darkness. He doesn't bother to close the car door, which bongs relentlessly into the night.

11

Liz sits on her couch with her laptop. She Googles Jack Harris. After retiring, Harris had briefly been a consultant to the FBI. He introduced the Seattle PD to "geographic profiling as a primary crime-solving tool." He utilized that profiling to nab four different serial killers. The latest being the Bellevue Butcher, who had become international news due to the horrifying and graphic nature of his crimes against teen runaways. She scrolls through the myriad headlines.

"Bellevue Butcher Shot Dead by Cop."

"Detective Jack Harris is being investigated for drinking on the job. His blood alcohol level was .08 at the time of the shooting."

"Criminal charges dropped against Jack Harris."

"Hero or criminal? Jack Harris retires from the Seattle PD."

Liz taps her pen on the page. She picks up her phone and dials. Harris answers groggily.

"Yeah! Hello?"

"Mr. Harris, this is Corporal Liz MacDonald. I am sorry to be calling you so late…"

Jack's voice cuts in and out. Bad cell service. "It's —ot a prob— I'm up. What can I h— you w—?"

"We seem to have a bad connection. Is it possible to meet tomorrow morning? I have a few follow-up questions. I can come to you."

"Sure, I'll pick you —the ferry to Long Harbour. They have one that— Vancouver at 10:00 AM. You —to walk down to Michelle's B&B, just —anyone—they let me use their dock as long —buy a coffee."

"Um, okay, I think I get that. Something about Michelle's B&B, Long Harbour. Tomorrow morning. Something about coffee. I'll see you then. Hello? Hello?"

The connection is broken. *Well*, she thinks, *nothing ventured, nothing gained. It isn't often you have a serial killer expert in your backyard.*

■ ■ ■

Amanda wakes, tied to a stainless steel fish-cleaning table with leather restraints, wearing nothing but her underwear. Her running shoes are still on. There are ropes, chains and tools hanging on the walls and rough wooden beams above her. The horror of her surroundings is so foreign, so impossible to comprehend, it takes a while to sink in.

Water is lapping below and light reflects from the water onto the rough beams and walls. A dismal foghorn sounds in the distance. Things slowly come into focus, saws, surgical instruments and scalpels on a table. Amanda gasps and begins to cry. She sees a man in scrubs, a butcher's apron and surgical gloves. He is wearing a respirator mask and goggles, which obscure his face, giving him an insect-like quality. He walks over to a video camera on a tripod and turns it on.

"For God's sake . . . what are you doing?"

He steps back to Amanda and languidly caresses her thigh, following her leg all the way down to her foot. Her eyes widen.

"No! Don't, please don't! Look, whatever I did, I'm sorry. Please, I'll do anything. Whatever you want."

He grabs heavier rubber gloves and slowly works his hands into them, one at a time.

"Of course you will. That's the beauty of it." The killer's voice is distorted by his mask.

He moves back to the makeshift surgical table, leans over her. Her eyes widen. He pauses and then turns on an mp3 player; "Flower Duet" from Delibes' *Lakmé* and angelic voices fill the room.

"I thought a little music would set the mood."

He slides the scalpel gently up her leg, not cutting her, almost a caress. She screams. He snips away her underwear. The killer leans over her helpless body.

"I suppose you think I'm going to kill you first, but what's the fun in that? No fun, really."

"Please, please, please . . . why are you doing this?"

"That is a very interesting question, Amanda. Why am I doing this? Some people say I'm crazy, that I lack a moral safety switch. Some might surmise I was abused as a child. But basically what it comes down to is, I *like* it! I like watching the different manifestations of pain. The interesting thing is there is really very little pain, comparatively speaking. At first, it's the mere horror of the thing . . . the inevitability of it all, and of course the blood loss, and the shock, which kills you in the end. Quite a fascinating process, really. Scream all you want by the way . . . It's just the two of us."

Amanda screams and screams again and screams until her larynx bursts, but the darkness of the north woods and black water swallow her cries.

■ ■ ■

Seagulls cry out as Liz runs along the seawall, pounding along, oblivious to the driving rain, as she rounds Siwash Rock, a small sea-stack like a lone sentinel in the fog between sea and forest. The air is filled with the lovely smell of salt and seaweed mixed with pine forest and wood smoke endemic to the Pacific Northwest. To Liz, running in the rain shows a commitment beyond the casual runner. A runner who is willing to run in soaked shoes and endure the dichotomy of shivering and sweating at the same time.

Liz pushes through, trying to quiet her mind for the meeting with Jack Harris. She knows if Ward or Richards finds out, she could face some form of a reprimand, if not worse. They did bring him in for questioning, after all. But she has to take risks if she wants to find a break in this case. In the big picture, helping find the answers to missing persons is the ultimate goal and, if a crime is involved, to bring that person to justice. She completes her loop around Stanley Park and heads back to her duplex along the waterfront. Once she gets on her block, she finishes up with a wind sprint, her flying feet slapping the wet pavement.

Liz enters her duplex, drenched; she takes off her shoes and sticks them on a rack to dry. She grabs a glass and gets some water from the kitchen faucet. She gulps it down and puts the glass in the sink. She heads up stairs, peeling her T-shirt off as she goes. She has to get a move on it if she wants to be on time. She grabs a towel from the linen closet, finishes undressing, wraps herself up. Dumps her panties and soggy running clothes into her hamper and heads into the shower.

Liz cranks the water up to scalding hot. Loosen up those tight muscles. She finishes off her shower by turning it to freezing cold. A trainer once told her the cold water helped wake up her biorhythms. She isn't sure she believes that but it seems to keep her energy up so she does it every day.

After she wraps up in a towel, she heads back to her bedroom. Her panties are on the floor. She picks them up then dumps them into the hamper.

Now dressed, Liz walks by the kitchen and notices the kitchen window is ajar, creating a small draft. Raindrops on the windowsill. She closes and locks it. She wipes the windowsill with a dishtowel. She grabs a cup of coffee in her eco-cup and leaves. If she's lucky, she'll just make the 10:00 AM ferry.

■ ■ ■

Jack picks up Liz at a Michelle's B&B dock in Long Harbour, on Saltspring Island—with whom he has an arrangement—a ten-minute walk from the BC Ferry terminal. She's wearing her uniform and a dark blue RCMP parka. She walks down the rickety, sloping ramp to the float where Jack's grungy aluminum tinner is tied up.

"Sorry about the walk," says Jack, handing her a large latte. "They won't let me tie up to the ferry dock. Only in Canada, eh?"

"No worries. We Canucks like our exercise. And our coffee. Thanks."

Jack starts the outboard. He heads out of Long Harbour, then turns north and opens up the throttle on the smooth water of the inlet. It's still raining, so they both put up the hoods of their rain parkas, and Liz is glad of the boat's canopy and the hot coffee. He takes the boat up the Trincomali Channel, making good time along the bulk of Galiano to the northeast, past Wallace and the Secretary Islands, past his own tiny island, to Valdes. Not much is said until they reach the shoreline where he found the foot. Jack points to the beach. The small creek, the dripping conifers, the rocky beach.

"That's where I found the foot. I can't say for certain if it washed up on the tide that morning, since I wasn't down this way the day before."

Liz snaps some photos with her phone. "Do you think it could have washed down the creek?"

"It's possible. Not much up there."

"Is there anything else you can tell me that might be helpful?"

"About finding the foot? No. How to investigate it? Yes."

"I'll take what I can get."

Jack turns the tinner around and heads back to his island, and pulls up to the dock. He jumps out and ties his boat up. Liz jumps onto the dock as well. She spots his sailboat, *Skookum*.

"Nice boat."

"She will be. Once I'm done restoring her. An old Lyle Hess design. I'm taking her up to Desolation Sound."

"I've never been. I hear it's beautiful."

Jack smiles. "It is."

"What's 'Skookum' mean?"

"Chinook word for Sasquatch."

"Bigfoot? Don't get me started . . ."

"Ah yes, the RCMP's working theory on feet."

"Not quite."

They walk up from the beach to his cabin. Jack opens the door. He and Liz enter, strip off their dripping rain gear, hang it in the mudroom. Jack stokes up the little woodstove, blowing on the embers.

On the table, Liz notes another empty Macallan, a half-eaten sandwich and more articles, maps and pictures of feet. Liz helps him pin up the photos on his wall as they talk.

"I thought you retired. Why are you working on this?"

"I'm good at it. Pretty much the *only* thing I'm good at."

"So why retire?"

"I shot a suspect."

"The Bellevue Butcher? Wasn't it a clean shoot?"

"Nope. I was drunk and turns out he was unarmed. But, drunk or sober, I would have shot that sonofabitch." Jack smiles. "According to IA, I'm an alcoholic with anger-management problems and a history of violence."

"A drunk and a misanthrope. Just my type."

"Flattery will get you everywhere. You seem to know all about me. Let me take a stab at your profile—Drunk dad, abused mom. Overachiever. College athletic scholarship was your ticket out. Pursued law enforcement to put abusers behind bars in a misguided attempt to find closure with your father."

Liz is taken aback by his accuracy. She curtly responds, "I studied criminology at Simon Fraser on a track scholarship."

"You're married to your job. You haven't got a boyfriend."

"That's none of your business."

"I'll take that as a no."

"What about you?"

"Divorced."

"There's a shocker." Liz picks up her picture from Jack's pile. "Is there a reason I'm on your wall?"

"You're my pinup of the month."

"Flattery will get you everywhere. So, purely hypothetically, if this *was* a serial killer…"

"Serial killer? I thought there was no foul play."

"Hypothetically . . ."

"Okay. What do we know? Start with what you *know*, not what you assume. You have thirteen feet, all in running shoes. You have the make and models of the shoes. So you know the longest each foot could have been in the water, based on the make and date of manufacture of the shoes and other factors."

"That doesn't narrow it down much."

"And you know RCMP's working theory," says Jack. "These are 'industrial accidents and suicides.' If so, why weren't they reported? Why aren't there floating feet in places with similar industries and geography, like Alaska or Russia? Or places with bridges like San Francisco or Portland?"

"I don't know."

"Now we're getting somewhere."

Liz looks at the map Jack has made detailing found foot locations. Jack points to the map.

"Typically, with geographic profiling, we could map out the places where the crimes occurred in order to determine the most likely area the killer lives or operates from . . ."

"But?"

"But in this case, we don't have any points of origin for the bodies or the crimes. Just locations where feet have been found."

"So how could we apply it here?"

"With the tides, these feet could float literally hundreds of miles."

"Great."

"Not so fast. They were all found on either full or dark moons. In other words, spring tides."

"Spring tides?"

"Extreme high or low tides. Full and dark moons. Wind and currents could be plotted. There are two periods of spring tides every month, more or less. Plus, other factors to figure in as well, such as offender type, hunting style, routines of the victims."

"We don't even know who the victims are."

"You don't because the killer doesn't want you to know who *he* is."

Liz's mobile phone buzzes. She signals to Jack that she has to take it.

"Liz MacDonald—hello? Hello? Can you hear me now?"

Jack motions her outside. "Go to the blue rock outside."

She grabs her jacket, steps outside, finds a medium-sized rock on the ground, spray-painted neon blue, shelters the phone from the rain.

"What? Okay, thanks Fouché, I'll be there as soon as I can . . . I said—Hello? Hello?"

Jack steps outside. Liz pockets her phone.

"I'm sorry. I have to go."

"Let me guess, another missing girl."

Liz looks at him hard. "Thanks for your help."

12

Liz drives to the crime scene, a desolate stretch of timbered road close to the beach south of Vancouver—salt marsh, overgrown trees and weeds outlining the road. Rain still spitting from lowering clouds, trees dripping and black along the road. The nearest house is half a mile away. Liz gets out of her car and puts on latex gloves. Richards and Fouché are wrapping up the crime scene as the victim's truck gets hitched to a tow truck. Liz catches the tow truck driver's attention.

"Hang on a minute, will you?"

Richards sees that Liz has arrived. "Hey, it's Footloose and Fancy-Free! Glad you could join us."

"Sorry I'm late. Please fill me in."

Richards consults his notebook: "Amanda Ferguson, white female, age twenty-three, at a beach party last night, left around midnight. An hour later, some kids found her truck parked here with the engine running, door open, no girl."

Liz looks inside the truck. She finds the girl's iPhone on the center console.

"Did you guys see this?"

Fouché looks at it. "Yeah. I jotted down her most recent calls so it can go to the lab."

She looks back at the passenger seat. There is a gym bag. Liz opens it. Inside it: a wallet, driver's license, hairbrush and cross-country uniform.

"This girl was abducted. She wouldn't leave her phone, wallet and ID." Liz holds up a brush. "Bag it, tag it and send it to the lab." Hands it to Fouché.

Richards says, "Who died and made you king of the world?"

"Oh, sorry. Just a suggestion. Didn't mean to step on any toes."

Richards looks at Fouché. "Bag it, tag it and send it to the lab."

Fouché grabs it and bags the brush. "Who knows what drunk kids do—maybe she's sleeping it off somewhere."

Richards adds, "Maybe she met up with a boy."

Liz is dubious. "But left her truck running?"

"Maybe he's really good in bed."

"He'd have to be the best lay in the world then. Do we know if she even has a boyfriend?"

"Well, if she was abducted, why didn't anyone at the party hear her scream?" Fouché asks.

"I don't know. Music playing? She was tasered?"

Liz's mobile vibrates. She steps away to answer it.

"This is Liz MacDonald."

"Liz, it's Jack."

"What's up?"

"You tell me. Wait, let me guess. You've got a missing girl, white, twenties, blonde. Probably a runner. You're sure it's an abduction but your colleagues think she's off with some boyfriend."

"How the hell did you know that?"

"Let me see the crime scene."

"Very funny. Not possible."

"Do you want to find the girl or not? You've lost about ten hours of the crucial first forty-eight and your partners don't even think she's missing. Tick, tock."

"Jack . . ."

"I'll take the early ferry tomorrow. You can fill me in then."

Liz disconnects the call and watches them tow Amanda's SUV away. She heads back to Richards and Fouché.

"Sorry about that. So where are we?"

"Nowhere," says Richards. "Send the truck to the crime lab. Track down her relatives and friends and see if they can shed any light on this. Trace her calls. Once we determine next-of-kin, we'll talk to them."

■ ■ ■

Classical music fills the air. Brahms' *Violin Concerto in D major*. Soothing music for the soul. The killer, in a now thoroughly blood-spattered disposable biohazard suit, breathing deeply of the music and the coppery smell of blood, wraps

Amanda's body—minus one foot—in a bloody, clear Visqueen sheet. Her lifeless eyes staring.

Runners have a special quality, he thinks as he admires his work. *They are fighters. They are half nuts. Who in their right mind ignores shin splints and their IT band to push through a seven-mile run? Runners.* That's why he loves them so much.

Their threshold for pain was so much greater. And then there was the horror on their faces when they realized what he was taking from them. It wasn't just their life. It was their ability to be free. Even if they held onto a sliver of hope that he wasn't going to let them bleed out, they would never again be able to run. It wasn't just any runner that fit the bill. He liked long-distance runners. Marathoners. Half-marathoners. Blond women who need that run to survive. To be able to blank whatever stresses they have running through their pretty little heads. The type of girl for whom running is oxygen. Who gets antsy if she can't go for a run.

Amanda was just that kind of girl. Pretty on the outside and a bundle of nerves on the inside. She needed the world to see how picture-perfect her world was but he saw the cracks in her facade. Facebook is brilliant for analyzing people in this new "Look at me" world. He had been watching her for some time. Her usual running routes ranged from the interior of Stanley Park to simple runs along the seawall. And she was easy to keep an eye on. She always wore something neon from Nike. Just do it! He loved stalking her. The running path his salt lick. The anticipation of what was to come made the actualization even more satisfying.

The look in her pleading eyes as she asked, "Please . . . I'll do anything."

He laughs. *Of course you will. How quickly they give that up. How delicious the moment when they realize that there is nothing they* can *do, though they will do* anything. *Offer up their bodies, their souls, anything at all to avoid the inevitable horror. The power of the inescapable.*

He softly caresses her cold thigh and follows it down to her calf. He lovingly touches the cleanly amputated stump where her foot had been. A beautiful Diana. Blond huntress of the Romans. The huntress was now the hunted. He enjoyed Amanda more than the others. She was unattainable, and yet here she is, lying lifeless on his table. Thankfully, he recorded everything so he can savor the moment again and again.

13

The night is quiet and Liz is asleep. She wakes suddenly. A noise coming from somewhere. Her back door? She takes a second to orient herself. Was she dreaming? There it is again, that same noise. Warily, she opens a small drawer in her nightstand, to get her heavy cop's flashlight, and a canister of pepper spray. With the light and the pepper spray held in front of her, she slowly creeps through her hallway, clearing each corner as she goes, just as she'd been trained. Sans gun, unfortunately. Once she gets to her kitchen, she sees that her kitchen window is ajar, banging slightly in the wind. She moves to the back door, unlocks it, and opens it suddenly. Her back gate is swinging and she hears footsteps running down the alley.

She rushes down the porch stairs and through her back gate but as she enters the alley, all she sees are shadows dancing on the garage doors and buildings.

Liz yells, "You better run, you sonofabitch!"

Liz comes back inside, slams and locks the door. "Dammit!"

She shuts the window and inspects the lock. Might be loose. She closes the curtain, breathing hard, her hands shaking.

■ ■ ■

Out in the flatlands east of Abbotsford—you could be in Kansas—Liz rings the bell of a small, weathered but reasonably well-maintained farmhouse. Liz is dreading this morning's interview. What can you say to the parents of a missing child? It's not natural and it shouldn't happen. A tired-looking woman answers the door. The haunted look in her eyes says it all.

"Mrs. Ferguson?"

"Yes?"

"I'm Corporal Liz MacDonald with the RCMP."

"Have you found her? She's not . . ."

"No. No, I'd just like to ask you a few questions about your daughter, to help us find her."

Mrs. Ferguson opens the door and Liz enters. She follows Mrs. Ferguson into their living room, which is simply done in a country style. Family pictures hang on the wall. Smiling faces of a happier time, pictures of Amanda with ribbons from various track meets. Mrs. Ferguson motions to a chair and Liz takes a seat. Amanda's father is there, watching TV. The constant drone of talking heads on a political news program bickering with each other blares in the background.

Amanda's mother looks at Liz, confused. "Those two other officers just left twenty minutes ago."

"I'm sorry. We don't always coordinate as we should. Do you remember their names?"

"No, but here's their card."

Liz glances at it. "I'm sorry, ma'am. We must have gotten our wires crossed. I didn't realize Richards and Fouché were already here to interview you."

"If you could even call it that. They made it out like Amanda was just a runaway."

"They told you she was a runaway?"

"Not in those exact terms but they implied that she may have run off without telling us. Amanda wasn't that kind of kid . . . Isn't."

"No, ma'am. I don't believe she is."

Mr. Ferguson, who appears to be staring at the TV screen, angrily shuts it off and turns to Liz. "Why isn't anyone taking this seriously? Amanda is a good girl. She's on the cross-country team. 'A' student. She doesn't drink or do drugs. She didn't have a fight with her boyfriend."

"They just got engaged," says Mrs. Ferguson. "It just doesn't make sense. She's not a runaway."

"It doesn't appear to be a runaway situation to me," says Liz. "I want you to know I am taking this seriously. Do you have her fiancé's name, address and phone number, please?"

"His name is Caleb Fraser. I'll go get his number."

"Also, do you have Amanda's hairbrush and tooth-brush?" No delicate way to ask about that. Amanda's mother breaks down.

"Oh my God."

Liz heads Mrs. Ferguson to the kitchen, gently guiding her to sit at the kitchen table. She sits across from her.

"I'm sorry. We just need to have some DNA just in case. I know it sounds horrible. But it can help eliminate her as a victim."

"I just . . ."

"Mrs. Ferguson, I will do everything in my power to find your daughter and bring you some kind of closure."

Wounded, Mrs. Ferguson looks at Liz hard. "*Closure?* What does that even mean? My daughter is gone. I don't know where she is or if she's ever coming home. What do *you* know about closure?"

Liz takes a deep breath. "I'm so sorry. You're right. I can't possibly know what you are going through."

■ ■ ■

Liz sits in her car, hands in her face. Frozen. Trying not to lose it. The words sound shallow but what else can you say? *Wouldn't it be a blessing if she were just a runaway?* She isn't and Liz knows that in her gut. *But maybe . . .* "Tick, tock," *as Jack says. Whatever it takes to find Amanda. Or bring justice to her killer.*

Liz breathes in deeply, looks up, straightens her rear-view mirror and starts the ignition.

■ ■ ■

Liz drives down a country road with Jack in the passenger seat. She stops the car and they get out. Liz walks Jack through the now-deserted crime scene.

"The beach party was down that trail. She supposedly left about midnight. Her SUV was found the next morning, engine running, here. Phone, wallet in the car. No girl. No sign of a struggle."

"Then she's been abducted."

"Yes."

Jack looks around carefully.

"What are you looking for?"

"I don't know. Something that doesn't fit. But I'll know it when I find it . . ."

As he says this, he kneels down and picks up something from the mud with his pen. It looks like a small tuft of cotton.

"What is it?"

"Looks like an animal tranquilizer dart. It's small so it must be from a pistol."

The metal dart has been squished flat into the tire tracks in the muddy road. Liz comes over and with a gloved hand picks it up and bags it.

"This might be how he subdued her."

Jack adds, "If we can analyze the tranquilizer, find what kind it is, where it's used—animal trainers, zookeepers, park rangers, etc.—we may have a lead."

"Jack, Bill Timmons worked for Vancouver Animal Control."

"Timmons?"

"The guy we picked up for the Stanley Park rapes . . . I need to drop this off at the lab. And then there is someone I think we should meet."

■ ■ ■

Liz is driving Jack through East Vancouver, the gritty skid-row section of town. Still drizzling and gray, of course. Some of the ramshackle buildings have been boarded up. Drug dens behind the boards. Trash is strewn on the street, while homeless, drug dealers and prostitutes mill about. It's where the hopeless go to die. Or at least disappear. In terms of prostitution, East Van is the end of the line. Liz watches Jack taking it all in.

"A veritable shopping mall for a serial killer," says Liz.

"It's good to be home. Pioneer Square is Seattle's version."

"That was the Bellevue Butcher's shopping grounds?"

"Pretty much. He also hit the Pacific Highway, but yeah."

Liz navigates her Jeep through the maze of streets and parks in front of a worn-down apartment building. She and Jack get out. She refers to her notebook before she rings the buzzer.

She buzzes and a gravelly voice answers. "What?"

"It's Corporal Liz MacDonald, RCMP. We spoke on the phone."

The buzzer unceremoniously lets them in. Once inside the building, they hike up three flights of stairs. On one of the landings there is the detritus of someone who sought shelter for the night. The smell is putrid: smoke, crack and urine.

Jack grimaces. "You take me to all the hot spots."

"Yeah, well, this lady may be on to something."

They climb to the apartment and Liz knocks on the door. Rosie George answers.

"Welcome." She opens the door. Her apartment is cluttered yet organized. The narrow hallway has stacks of banker's boxes full of files from floor to ceiling, each representing a missing person. Scattered throughout are knickknacks bearing twelve-step slogans such as "One day at a time," "Live and let God" and "I'm not going to give anybody free rent in my head." Also taped along the walls are pictures of missing women with the dates of their disappearances and names of their parents and/or children. The most recent picture is of Amanda. Rosie gives them the once-over and points between the two.

"So what do we have here, the PR gal and her alcoholic boyfriend?"

"No, I'm Canadian Mountie Barbie, and he is not my boyfriend. Rosie George, meet Jack Harris, formerly with the Seattle PD."

"What makes you think I'm an alcoholic?" says Jack.

"I can smell it on you, cowboy."

"Takes one to know one."

"Damn straight." Rosie smiles, takes a drag on her cigarette. "My worst day sober is better than my best day high."

Jack refers to one of her posters. "So I've read. Should we recite the Serenity Prayer now?"

Liz steps in, not wanting this to go off the rails. "Rosie, before this turns into a camp meeting, we'd like to talk to you about the Missing-Missing."

"What do you want to know? How people go missing or how RCMP does nothing about it?"

"Let's start with the missing. Who are they and why do you think they are missing?"

"In the past four years, my blog has posted a list of over sixty women who have gone missing in Vancouver and the Lower Mainland."

Rosie lights another cigarette as she continues, turns to her computer, clicks on a link to her blog with a slide show of missing women.

Jack looks at the pictures. "Christ . . ."

From a file drawer, Rosie pulls out file after file.

"Of those sixty, I narrowed that down to about forty, after eliminating ODs, suicides, and gang contacts. From that, a dozen have been located, some dead. That leaves us with a list of twenty-two young, healthy, athletic women who have simply vanished."

Jack refers to the photos. "They're all blondes."

"Very observant. Seattle's finest?"

Liz pulls out the file on Amanda from the stack.

"Rosie, what do you know about this case? Amanda Ferguson doesn't seem to fit the East Vancouver profile. She's not one of the 'Missing-Missing.'"

Rosie takes a long drag on her cigarette. "She's gone and I don't think she's ever coming back."

"What makes you say that?" asks Jack.

"Because of the twenty-one other missing women who match her description."

"She could have run off with her boyfriend," says Liz.

"Buggered off and left her truck running?"

"How do you know that?"

"I have my sources."

Jack interjects, "Do you have a list of the last-seen locations for the probable twenty-two?"

Rosie points Jack to her map with the corresponding thumbtacks.

"I have mapped out home addresses and 'last-seens.'"

Jack takes a step back and takes the map in. Steps up and makes a couple of circles with a pen.

"Okay, if you compare last-seens to where the feet are turning up, there could be a connection. Possibly down the Fraser. There are way too many people going missing from the same area."

Rosie lights another cigarette. "This is just a little too reminiscent of the Pickton pig farm killings."

"Don't bring that up, for God's sake," Liz responds.

"That bothers you? It should. It's an inconvenient truth that the RCMP *and* Vancouver PD ignored evidence because the abducted girls were drug addicts and prostitutes. If it were West Van girls, it'd be a different story."

"Hey. I'm an East Van girl. I grew up on Hastings Street. And I still live in East Van. We take all crimes seriously."

"You don't look like an East Van girl."

"Not everyone ends up on the streets."

"Congratulations, your parents must be very proud."

"Rosie, I'm here because I think you are onto something."

"Fine, but RCMP isn't getting the warning out."

"We don't want to create mass panic."

"That's what they said with Pickton. That bastard kidnapped, tortured, and raped almost fifty women, turned them into sausages and fed them to his pigs. Fed the pigs to his buddies. While you did nothing! Some of those women were my friends. Maybe if there'd been a mass panic, they'd still be alive."

"I'm so sorry, Rosie. But Vancouver PD had the lead on that case and technically they have jurisdiction over Stanley Park."

"If you're so sorry, then don't make excuses. If Vancouver has jurisdiction, why were you sent in to nab Timmons?"

"It was a joint task force and since I'm a blond runner . . ."

"So two agencies screwed that up. RCMP has the sole lead on the Highway of Tears up in Hazelton and has been doing *such* a bang-up job on that."

"I get your point, Rosie. You think we ignore the disenfranchised. But I promise you, the RCMP will do whatever it takes to make sure that doesn't happen again."

"I'll believe it when I see it."

"Is it possible to get copies of the files you have on your probable twenty-two?"

"What? You don't have your own files? Of course not. I have everything on each girl on my website. Click on their names—all the documents are there. If I get any new info, I'll call you."

"Thanks, Rosie. I'll do my best."

■ ■ ■

Back on the street, Liz and Jack walk to Liz's car.

Jack shakes his head. "That went well."

"Rosie is a trip. Give me a second, I have to check in with headquarters." She checks her pockets. "Damn, I must have left my phone."

As they approach her car, Liz sees the broken glass and shattered window.

"Ah, shit. This is just my week."

She opens the door. Sweeps out the glass.

"Anything missing?"

"Looks like some CDs. They left my phone."

Her cell phone is still on the seat. Jack looks at it. He picks up the phone.

"It's weird they wouldn't take your phone."

"Yeah . . . Junkies aren't exactly known for their powers of observation."

She carefully brushes glass shards off of her seat.

"Come on. You can just catch the ferry."

■ ■ ■

Liz drives Jack to the ferry in Tsawassen. The parking lot is empty and the gray sky is turning darker as the sun sets. A cold wind blows across the puddles in the parking lot. She pulls her Jeep into the lot, turns off the engine. There is a long pause.

Liz breaks the silence. "So . . ."

"Quite a day," says Jack.

"Do you really think this is Pickton all over again?"

"Only that the RCMP is making the same investigative mistakes."

"What would you do?"

"I don't know . . . Yet. Want to grab a drink and talk it through?"

"Sorry, I don't drink."

"You don't think much of people who do."

"You wouldn't either if you knew my father."

"I'm sorry to hear that."

"Have you ever considered AA?" Liz asks.

"Have you ever been in a room with those weenies? My worst day drunk is better than my best day in AA."

"Point taken. I really do appreciate your help on this, though."

"Call me if you need anything. Let me work on these files."

For some reason, there is an awkward moment. It feels like the end of a date rather than an investigation. Jack leans in—is he about to peck her on the cheek? Liz quickly shoves her hand out to shake his. Then at the last second, leans in and gives him an unexpected peck on the cheek.

"Thanks, Jack. I really appreciate your help."

"Sure. Just professional courtesy, ma'am."

Jack walks away toward the ferry absently touching his cheek, as if he had just been slapped.

14

Jack sits on his front porch, nursing his second single-malt, thinking over the day's events. Handel's "Sarabande", plays on his iPod. It has been a while since he has been on a hunt.

The mistake so many investigators make is coming to conclusions too quickly. Preconceived conclusions cloud the process and you can miss clues that are right in front of you the whole time. It's a form of confirmation bias where you look only at evidence that bolsters your hypothesis and ignore contradictory evidence. Bias happens to everyone. The trick is knowing it does, and not allowing yourself to fall into the pitfalls. He would not make that mistake. He takes another slug of whiskey, the smoky peatyness scouring the back of his throat in a pleasant Scottish fashion.

Jack notices a light on in a cabin on a small island across the bay. Probably the caretaker's cabin. This time of year, he is the only one living on that island. While he's watching, a second light appears on the other end of the island. Jack takes a pair of binoculars off a hook, focuses on the second light: a cabin, possibly, tucked back in the trees.

■ ■ ■

Liz is exhausted. But she knows sleep won't come. She turns on her computer to work on Rosie's files. She taps into the RCMP database. She looks at picture after picture of the missing girls. Twenty-two photos—all blond, all runners. That can't be a coincidence.

"Where are you?" Almost a whisper. A plea.

She looks at her wall. She looks at the map with the twenty-two red pins representing where each woman was last seen. She goes back to Rosie's blog. Under a photo of Amanda from the UBC cross-country team:

Well, RCMP is ignoring it again. Another missing girl. God forbid they think crime actually happens in Vancouver. We wouldn't want the world to know about our seedy underbelly of gangs, drug trafficking and serial murder. Might drop the property values! Can't let that happen—the average detached home in Greater Vancouver is worth over $1.3 million! That's a lot of money for 1,200 square feet. And let's not forget, tourism brings in billions—not millions, BILLIONS—of dollars to Vancouver. Wouldn't want that golden goose to dry up courtesy of a few missing girls and some floating feet. They want me to drop it.

But I will not let it drop! This will not remain covert. Another girl has gone missing. ANOTHER! Amanda Ferguson disappeared. She was celebrating her engagement to Caleb Fraser with friends at a beach bonfire. What could be more innocent that that? Roasted marshmallows and good times. Or so you would think . . . Amanda's SUV was found with the engine still running but no Amanda. RCMP claims she may have run off to hook up with some guy. But left her engine running? That doesn't even make sense. I don't know about you but when I run off for a roll in the hay, I generally shut my car off. Blame the victim as always. Good job RCMP, as per usual.

■ ■ ■

Liz has fallen asleep at her desk. Something wakes her with a small start. She hears a noise coming from her back door. *Again? Shit.* Warily, she walks through the room. There it is again, that same noise. She continues through the kitchen; she listens outside the back door, unlocks it and opens it suddenly. There's nothing there. Just the wind.

She turns back into the room and *thwack!* Something slaps her neck, stinging sharply. A small dart, a tuft of colored cotton on the end. Liz struggles to stay upright but the world spins, goes dark and she tries to raise herself as a vague shadow approaches . . . consciousness slips away from her like water through her hands.

■ ■ ■

Liz wakes slowly. She sits up and screams. She's in the middle of a rainforest, wearing nothing but her underwear, in a dripping, cold, fog-shrouded wilderness of huge old-growth trees. Stanley Park perhaps—or someplace more remote. Horrified, she finds the small tranquilizer dart still stuck in her neck, which she pulls out, groggy from the drug. She staggers up, clutching herself, stumbles, shivering. It's freezing cold and raining. She is not bound.

She sees a hooded figure through the trees and fog, moving slowly toward her. Panicking, she stumbles to her feet and runs—the figure chases her through the trees. She runs faster, leaping over logs and boulders, her natural speed kicking in—cutting her bare feet on sharp stones sticking up through the moss, not caring—but now she runs into a bog, slowing her as she splashes through the mud—the man chasing her closes in.

Liz struggles to run through the mud and just as she seems to be getting an edge, a steel cable comes tight around her ankle and she falls flat—the man is almost on her—she wrestles to free the cable but it's locked tight on her ankle as the man descends on her with a huge meat cleaver and she holds up her hands and screams.

■ ■ ■

Liz wakes with a start in her own apartment, right where she fell asleep the night before, sitting at her computer. She gasps for air. Stares at the ceiling. She vomits into a wastebasket. Resigned, she gets up, drinks a handful of water at the kitchen sink, turns to her treadmill. She turns it on slow, hops on and begins jogging. Liz turns it up faster. She runs hard now. But it's not fast enough or hard enough. Liz turns it up even faster, feet pounding the spinning mat. She runs harder. She turns it up even faster. She turns it to the highest setting, sprinting full bore. She stumbles and shuts it down. She leans over, breathing hard. Totally spent. She shakes everything off, gets back on the treadmill and begins to run again.

■ ■ ■

He listens to her voice. It soothes him after a particularly stressful day.

"*Please, please, please . . . why are you doing this?*

"*That is a very interesting question, Amanda. Why am I doing this? Some people say I'm crazy, that I lack a moral safety switch. Some might surmise I was abused as a child. But basically what it comes down to is, I* like *it! I like watching the different manifestations of pain. The interesting thing is there is really very little pain comparatively speaking. At first, it's the mere horror of the thing . . . the inevitability of it all, and of course the blood loss and the shock, which kills you in the end. Quite a fascinating process, really. Scream all you want, by the way . . . It's just the two of us.*"

The video rewinds and plays again.

"*Please, please, please . . .*"

"*Scream all you want . . . It's just the two of us.*"

And scream she does. The video plays as the killer cheerfully washes the blood off the fish-cleaning table. He is meticulous, even using a toothbrush and a cotton swab to get inside the cracks of the table. He sprays the table with Luminol.

It's wonderful: if you are prepared, you can basically get away with murder. On Amazon you can buy a Luminol kit. Blood spatter? Yep, better clean up a little more. Watch a couple of crime shows and you have a textbook of how to avoid detection. He loves watching crime shows to see how stupid people are. *It's unbelievable the dumb things people do. Like the guy who wore gloves during a burglary but took them off to take a swig out of a whiskey bottle, leaving a fingerprint.* Not him. He is always careful.

He picks up a UV light. A couple of specks still left. He grabs his toothbrush and scrubs some more.

He finishes and opens up a mini-fridge and grabs a sandwich, which is right next to a Ziploc bag containing Amanda's severed foot and running shoe. He sits to devour the sandwich, watching his home video, as Amanda screams. *Delicious.*

15

Liz sips her coffee at the conference table. She is looking through different files when Fouché walks in.

"You look tired," he says.

"Is that a polite way of saying I look like shit?"

"Your words, not mine. But you do look worse for wear."

"Didn't get much sleep last night."

Richards walks in. Liz turns to him. "By the way, I went to interview the Fergusons and turns out, you guys had already been there."

"Oh, I'm sorry," says Richards. "I didn't know I needed your permission."

"It's not that. We need to coordinate better."

Fouché says, "Actually, that's my fault. I thought we should get a jump on this."

Liz shrugs it off. "Okay. When are we questioning the fiancé?"

"Us, not you," says Richards. "You can observe. He should be in the interrogation room by now."

The three head to the interrogation room. Liz and Ward observe through the two-way mirror. Seated at the table is Caleb Fraser. He looks haggard and now older than his twenty-two years.

Richards opens. "Thank you for meeting with us, Caleb. We'll try to make this as painless as possible. State your name and address."

"Caleb Fraser. 2015 Discovery Street, Vancouver V7126I."

"What is your relationship with Amanda?"

"She is my fiancée."

"Where were you when Amanda disappeared?"

"I was at the party until one. My friend drove me home and I slept. It wasn't until her parents called me in the morning that I realized she hadn't made it home."

"Do you two live together?"

"No, she still lives with her folks. They thought she'd stayed with me and I thought she went home."

"When was the last time you saw Amanda?"

"Amanda left the party around midnight."

"Were you drinking?"

"I had a few, yeah."

"Are you a habitual drug user?"

"What? No!"

"Drugs? Pot? Ecstasy?"

"Just a little pot sometimes. I'll be honest, people were smoking pot at the party."

Richards writes on his tablet as he speaks. "Habitual . . . drug . . . user."

"Was Amanda using?"

"No. She doesn't touch the stuff. She doesn't want anything to affect her running."

Fouché stares at Caleb intently. "We will need a list of the people at the party to confirm your alibi."

He pushes a tablet and pen towards him.

"No problem."

"How many people were at the party?"

"About fifteen."

"Why didn't you leave together?"

"She had a cross-country meet the next day and I wanted to stay longer."

"Why didn't you walk her to her car?"

Caleb voice rises. "Don't you think I wish I had?"

"Did you have a fight with Amanda?"

"No."

"Did you cheat on her?"

"No. Never."

"Did she cheat on you?"

"No! We were celebrating our engagement!"

"Awfully young to be getting married."

"I'm not too young to know who I love."

"You don't think it's odd that you and your fiancée left at different times at your engagement party?"

"I told you, she had a meet and wanted to go to bed earlier."

"Why have the party the night before a big meet then?"

"I don't know. Her friends planned it."

Fouché steps in. "Where did you get the tranquilizer darts, Caleb?"

"What?!"

"Tranquilizer dart. Is that how you subdued her?"

"Amanda loves me. Why would I have to subdue her to come with me?"

Richards and Fouché glance at each other and leave.

■ ■ ■

Richards and Fouché confer with Ward and Liz. Liz watches Caleb through the mirror.

Ward says, "He's got a point."

Fouché points to him through the mirror. "It's the boyfriend."

Richards agrees. "It's always the boyfriend."

"Unless it's the husband," says Fouché.

Ward steps in. "We have nothing to hold him on."

Liz shakes her head. "It's not him. He speaks of her in the present tense. You didn't trick him into anything because he is telling the truth. Let me talk to him."

Richards shrugs. "Have at it."

■ ■ ■

Liz enters the interrogation room with a cup of coffee.

"I hope you like cream and sugar. Caleb, my name is Corporal Liz MacDonald."

Caleb accepts the coffee but looks at Liz warily.

"Thanks." He takes a sip of the coffee. "I know you're trying to get my DNA. I've watched *Forensic Files*. If you wanted it, just ask. I've got nothing to hide."

"I'm trying to find Amanda. Can you think of anyone who might want to hurt Amanda?"

"No, everyone loved her."

"Did she date anyone before you who might be upset or jealous?"

"Maybe. She mentioned some guy she dated a few years ago."

"Do you know his name?"

"No. They broke up two years ago and she never wanted to talk about it."

"Can you remember anything she may have said about him?"

"He worked for the city in some capacity."

"Do you know what he did for the city?"

"Some official-type job."

"Why did they break up?"

"She said he was weird."

"Weird how?"

"Possessive. Controlling. He didn't want her on Facebook. He didn't like her major in school. So she got fed up and they broke up. Then weird things started happening. She felt like someone was stalking her. She knew it was him."

"Stalking her? Did she report it to the police?"

"No, she thought he would go away eventually."

"They never do. Did he e-mail her? Call her?"

"Not since we've been together. That I know of anyway."

"What do you mean?"

"Amanda is a pretty private person. I'm not saying she hides things from me but, you know, sometimes she doesn't share every little thought."

"Don't you think if he did something she would tell you?"

"I would hope so. But if bad things happen, she isn't one to dwell on it."

"Thank you, Caleb. I'll do my best to find her."

■ ■ ■

Liz steps out to consult with Ward, Richards and Fouché.

"We need to track down the other boyfriend," says Liz. "He's our only lead."

Fouché shakes her off. "What's wrong with the current boyfriend?"

"He didn't do it. The first guy was a stalker."

Richards adds, "It's *always* the boyfriend."

"So you said. But which one? We should track down the ex. Start with phone records, e-mails. Talk to her girl-friends—they may remember him."

Richards smiles wryly. "I'm on it, boss."

Liz covers. "Sorry, sir. I was speaking generally, not directing traffic."

Fouché asks, "What about Timmons?"

Ward steps in, adamant. "Off-limits. Besides, we have nothing to link him to Amanda but conjecture."

Fouché counters, "Timmons is the Stanley Park Rapist. We just don't have enough to indict him. But— "

"And so we have even less than nothing to get him for Amanda's disappearance," says Ward. "Do we have the lab report on that tranquilizer dart?"

Richards consults his little pad. "Yes. It's etorphine hydrochloride. Used to subdue large animals."

Liz adds, "Vancouver Animal Control uses it on bears and cougars."

Ward is resolute. "Not enough to get a warrant."

"Seriously?" says Liz.

"But we know Amanda Ferguson dated someone who worked for the city. Timmons worked for Animal Control, for God's sake!" says Fouché.

"So? She could have been dating a garbage-man, for all we know."

Richards steps in. "No, Liz is right. It's too compelling."

Liz adds, "We need to search Timmons' apartment."

Ward considers and turns to Liz. "Not we. Let me see if I can get a warrant, but Liz, you are out of it."

■ ■ ■

Ward, Richards, Fouché and three RCMP constables approach a stout brick single-family home. It is well-maintained, though the design seems outdated and out of character for a single man. Window boxes with cheery orange marigolds and a garden gnome by the doorstep. Ward bangs on the door.

"RCMP! We have a warrant to search your premises."

Timmons answers the door, looking like he hasn't slept. "Let me see it."

Ward hands him the warrant. Timmons examines the warrant and nonchalantly opens the door for everyone to enter.

"Welcome to my humble abode."

"Thank you, sir. Please step outside and wait here with the constable."

Timmons steps outside. Takes out his cell phone. "Make yourselves at home. I'm calling my lawyer."

The interior decor, much like the exterior, belies the fact a thirty-year-old man owns it. There are cross-stitched pillows and floral upholstered furniture. It is extremely tidy and everything in perfect order. Fouché does a quick search on Timmons' computer. In his browser history,

Fouché finds perverse fetish and bondage websites—disturbing enough: women—and sometimes men—in leather, bound and gagged in demeaning postures, being whipped and tortured in various ways. The other constables systematically go through drawers, cabinets and bookshelves. One opens the closet and finds a Ketch-All, an animal control pole with a noose on the end, gives it to Richards.

Fouché picks up a photo of Timmons. Timmons and an older man smiling at the camera. The background looks like the Gulf Islands and there is a boathouse and a distinctive totem pole. Fouché takes a photo of it with his phone.

Ward pops her head into the room. "Anything?"

Richards holds up the Ketch-All.

Ward is disappointed. "He would need that for his job." She looks to Fouché. "Anything else?"

"Just some porn on his computer."

Richards is hopeful. "Kiddie porn?"

"No. Bondage stuff. Creepy."

Ward sighs. "We can't bust him for that. It's not illegal to be a creep."

■ ■ ■

The search is wrapping up and Timmons is patiently waiting outside, sitting on his front porch steps smoking a cigarette, talking on his cell phone.

Fouché approaches him casually. "You have some interesting tastes in photography."

"Nothing illegal in having interesting taste."

"No there's not. So were you doing anything interesting on Saturday night?"

"Talk to my lawyer." Timmons hands him his phone.

■ ■ ■

Liz showers after her evening run. She ran ten miles. Longer than her usual but she needed extra time to think—or not think, more to the point. The hot water relaxes her tight muscles. She finishes it off with a shot of freezing cold water. Liz exits her bathroom in a bathrobe and a towel wrapped around her head. She peers through a slat in her blinds. Nothing. No dream this time.

Liz shakes it off and takes the towel off of her head. Loud knocking rattles her door. She looks through the peephole. She doesn't see anything. Suddenly a face appears in the peephole. Liz jumps. It's Fouché. She undoes the chain-lock and opens the door.

"Doug? What's up?"

"Hey Liz, sorry. I wanted to give you the update on the Timmons' search. But we can speak later if it's a bad time."

"Richards filled me in."

"I think Timmons could be good for it."

"What? The rapes?"

"The feet."

"Seriously? I thought you didn't like him for that."

"There's something about him. I asked him where he was Saturday and he clammed up. Look at this."

Fouché pulls out his cell phone and shows Liz the picture of Timmons in the Gulf Islands with the boathouse and totem pole behind him.

"This looks like the Gulf Islands. Isn't it a coincidence how two feet have shown up there?"

"In crime, there is no such thing as coincidence."

"Sherlock Holmes?"

"Jack Harris."

"Harris? Are you talking with him? Ward was very clear on keeping him out of this."

"She also said to keep an eye on him. He's an expert on serial murders. I'm consulting with him."

"Can I come in? We need to talk about this."

"I'm just getting ready for bed. I have an early morning run before work."

"Oh, sorry. Of course."

Liz refers to the picture. "We need to search property records in the Gulf Islands. Maybe we can link Timmons that way. Can you e-mail me that pic?"

"Ah, sure. Right. See you tomorrow."

■ ■ ■

It's a misty morning in Stanley Park. Dew droplets sprinkle Liz's fleece. Liz sets her watch and begins her run. She never runs with music—it distracts her from the natural rhythm of her running. To Liz, music is a cheat. She prefers using her own grit to push herself rather than a fast song. That, and it affects situational awareness. Liz sees countless cute young girls running with ear buds. It just screams, "I can't hear you if you come after me." *Better to run in silence*, she thinks.

She runs by the first-growth cedars, over the footbridge. She hesitates at the side trail, still ominous with mist and shadows. She pauses, turns to look behind her. No one is there. She takes a deep breath and runs onto the side trail. As she runs, she hears footsteps behind her. She glances over her shoulder and briefly sees a man jogging behind her through the trees—but closing. She quickens her pace. The man runs faster. She hurdles a fallen tree.

She sprints full-out and finally bursts onto the regular jogging path on the crowded seawall. Spent, she turns and looks behind her. A harmless-looking man in a hoodie jogs past her.

"Get it together, Liz," she says to herself. She heads back down to the seawall to do some wind sprints, hoping that will clear her head.

16

Knifeblade Bob, a wild-haired, bearded man in a ratty gray Cowichan sweater, comes out of the trees and steps onto the shingle of a small, stony beach on Francisco Island in the Gulf Islands. The man is known as Knifeblade Bob because he wears four or five knives of various kinds—sheath knives, folding hunters, simple pocket knives—on his belt or in his pockets. A yellow Lab runs eagerly ahead, a big stick in her mouth.

"Daisy! Wait for me, girl!"

Daisy stops at something that has washed ashore, among the kelp and assorted flotsam. She drops her stick. Pushes it with her nose, digging, and then whines. She looks up with a sad, mournful look.

"Daisy? What do you have there? Did you find a shoe, girl? What are you going to do with a shoe?"

It is a shoe. A running shoe. Knifeblade Bob takes out one of his knives, turns over the shoe, revealing a decaying human foot within, the anklebone protruding. He recoils.

"Christ!"

The dog whines again after she sees the foot. She barks. He pets his dog. "It's okay girl. It'll be okay."

■ ■ ■

Liz arrives at work, eco-coffee cup and briefcase in hand. On her desk is a single running shoe with a Post-It note attached: "If the shoe fits!" She hears Richards snickering from the other end of the conference table.

"Very funny, Frank."

"Hey Liz, what do you call a blonde with an IQ of a 100?"

"A foursome. You need new jokes, Frank. They're older than you."

"Liz, I got a personal question. How come you always wear that paracord bracelet? It's a real fashion statement."

She looks at the black, woven paracord bracelet on her wrist. "Well, you never know when you might need ten feet of really strong line. I might have to tie you up some day."

"I can't wait. Is today the day?"

"In your dreams."

Liz settles in and researches Amanda Ferguson's social media sites. She peruses pictures of her smiling with friends and teammates, including the two she posted the night of her disappearance. Her last post: "Can't wait for tomorrow's meet at UBC! Go, Thunderbirds!"

She looks back at photos from two to three years prior and there are no pictures of anyone who might be a boyfriend.

Fouché approaches Liz. Puts his hand on her shoulder. She jumps.

"Sorry. Little jumpy, aren't you?"

"I haven't been getting much sleep."

"Really. You don't look so good."

"Don't you mean 'You look tired'?"

"Po-tay-toe, Po-tah-toe."

"Gosh, thanks. I may have a stalker. I think someone may have creeped my place the other day. Plus, my car was broken into."

"Was it Timmons?"

"I have no idea."

"Why didn't you say something?"

"What's to say? I filed a report."

"Do you want me to get a patrol car to drive by your place at night?"

"No. That won't be necessary."

"Liz, didn't you say they never go away? You are a single, good-looking, blond female runner. Right on this guy's victim profile. If you're on his radar . . ."

"Maybe you're right. I'll look into getting a patrol." She looks at the file Fouché is holding. "What've you got?"

"You first."

"It's weird. This girl was an avid Facebook user but during the three months she was dating the mystery man, she posted next-to-no photos on Facebook, and none with any guys in them."

"Maybe she wasn't into social media then."

"Seems like a strange gap. I want to try and run down some of her friends and see if they have any more information. What's in the file?"

"We just got a call about another foot in the Gulf Islands. The guy who found it is named Bob Carter. Oddly enough, it was right across from where the last one was found. On an island called Francisco. Within sight of Jack Harris's place."

"Really? I'm on it. You coming?"

"Sorry, can't," says Fouché. "I'm swamped researching property records." He dumps the file on her desk.

Liz opens the file. She looks at the photo of the foot. She taps her mouse and scrolls over the cross-country picture of Amanda. She picks up her phone.

"Zach. It's Liz MacDonald. Did you get foot number fourteen in yet? Okay, when you do, can you run the DNA on Amanda's hairbrush and look for a match? Call me if you get a hit. Thanks!"

Liz calls Jack on her cell as she is leaving. "Jack, can you hear me? Foot fourteen just turned up. Right in your backyard. Literally."

■ ■ ■

Jack, on his cell, by the blue rock outside his cabin, is watching the police activity across the water. Boats with flashing lights.

"Yeah, I can see it from here. It's on Francisco Island, a small private island with a dozen summer houses. Pretty deserted this time of year."

"I have to interview the guy who found it," says Liz. "His name is Bob Carter."

"You mean Knifeblade Bob? I know him. He's been the caretaker over there for years. You'll love him."

"*Knifeblade*? I'm sure I will. After, I'm going to try to interview some of the locals."

"Who's with you?"

"No one."

"So you are going to go door-to-door, alone, on an isolated island where someone may be cutting off people's feet."

"I take your point."

"I'll meet you at the B&B in Long Harbour, on Salt Spring." Jack hangs up and pockets his phone. He heads back to his cabin.

■ ■ ■

Jack picks Liz up at the B&B dock. She smiles as she sees him, walks down the float and takes the obligatory latte from Jack. It's a dank, cold, misty day, the wind-chill cutting right through her parka. She hunkers down beside him under the canopy and Jack guns it up the channel, the short steep wavelets slapping the aluminum hull.

As they approach the island, Jack says, "That's Francisco Island right there. It's essentially uninhabited right now, as far as I know, except for Knifeblade Bob. Just a few summer homes owned by people from the mainland."

"Any reason to think your pal Knifeblade is involved?"

"No. He's eccentric but not crazy. You'll see."

■ ■ ■

Liz and Jack land on the small gravel beach and stroll up to a wooden cabin with lots of moose and deer antlers accenting the entrance. Wind chimes made out of animal bones and sea debris hang in nearby trees and the eaves of the cabin like weird DNA.

Liz points to the mobile made of bones. "So you're sure he's not crazy?"

Jack laughs her off. Daisy, Knifeblade Bob's yellow Lab, bounds up to Jack, greeting him. She drops a ball she had in her mouth. Jack pets her.

"Hello, Daisy. Who's a good girl?"

He picks up the ball and tosses it. She bounds off to get it. Knifeblade walks out of his cabin.

"Get your own damn dog, Jack!"

Jack looks at Bob standing in his doorway. "Bob. Good to see you. This is Corporal Liz MacDonald with the RCMP."

"Howdy. Jack, are you working the case?"

"No, just helping a friend."

Bob takes them inside.

■ ■ ■

Knifeblade's shack is littered with strange jetsam and bones with a custom knife-making set-up in a corner. He begins to whittle with a very large knife as they interview him.

Uncomfortable, Liz looks at Bob and his knife. "Would you mind putting that knife away, sir?"

"No, not at all."

He puts the knife away and pulls out another one from his belt, a distinctive, one-of-a kind custom-made knife, and continues to whittle.

"Sir, pardon me, but what is with the knives?"

Bob holds up the knife. "Is this a dagger which I see before me, the handle toward my hand? Come, let me clutch thee." He smiles at Liz and continues, "In close quarters, I'd take a knife over a gun any day. They are precise. Crisp, clean, primitive, yet efficient. The purity of steel. Man's first step out of the Stone Age. And, you never run out of bullets. I made this one myself from a piece of stainless steel 440-C bridge cable." He hands it to Liz, who looks at it without touching it.

"Fascinating. Please put it away."

He smiles, wipes the blade and puts it in a sheath on his belt.

Liz glances at Jack. "Bob, we'd like to ask you some questions about the foot you found."

"I'd like to know what kind of monster would do this to someone."

"Actually, we don't know there was foul play."

"Foul play or not, Daisy hasn't been the same since."

"I'm not surprised. They say dogs can get PSTD too. They see it all the time in military dogs."

Knifeblade Bob looks concerned. "My girl!"

Jack covers. "I'm sure Daisy'll get over it."

"I hope so." He pets Daisy's head.

Liz continues, "Is there anything else you can tell us that might be helpful?"

"Yeah. I know who did it."

"Excuse me?"

"I know who did it."

"Please don't say it's Bigfoot."

"Bigfoot? What kind of nut do you think I am?" He pauses for dramatic effect. "It's Al-Qaeda."

"Al-Qaeda."

"Al-Qaeda has been infiltrating Canada for years. Over 300,000 people enter our country every year. Refugees come in all the time with fraudulent documents. What percentile of that are terrorists?

"I have no idea."

"They can easily sneak in undetected and mingle with Vancouver's Pakistani community. Nobody around on these small islands in the winter. Think about it. We have a porous border. Remember the guy who took a ferry to Port Washington with a car full of explosives? The Millennium Bomber? There are cells everywhere."

Liz glances at Jack.

"Yeah, but why would they be severing feet?"

Bob says matter-of-factly, "They're getting rid of drug dealers who can link them to cells. They're probably getting rid of hands and teeth too so you can't identify the bodies but those don't float like the feet. I've seen lights at night and boats coming and going at all hours."

Jack's interest is piqued. "Around here? On the island?"

"Yeah. All the time."

"Tell me more about those lights, Bob."

"I'll show you. Let's go for a walk. Daisy! Walkie!" Daisy jumps up, barking.

■ ■ ■

Outside, there is a slight breeze, making the flotsam, jetsam and bone mobiles chime eerily. Knifeblade shows them around the island with Daisy. It is hauntingly beautiful in the gray, misty afternoon—and deserted. Black, black ravens caw at them from red-barked arbutus trees as they walk along a trail through the timber, pale light shining through the mist, past boarded-up summer cabins. A painted sign warns of recent wolf activity on the island.

"Wolves?" says Liz. "Seriously?"

"You betcha!" says Knifeblade. "Got our own pack, swam over from Valdes and Vancouver Island, I reckon. Ate just about every deer on the island. Pretty much gone now, though. They never bothered me. We do have bears, however. Sometimes they break into the houses looking for food. I run 'em off."

"Wolves, Al-Qaeda, and bears, oh my," says Liz. "What next!"

"Don't ever say what next," says Knifeblade.

They walk up a sloping ridge to a cliff, overlooking a wide cove with a gravel beach, about a half a mile down the island. A few cabins and cottages can be seen scattered through the trees, just back from the beach.

"These are all summer homes. Eighteen all together on the island. It's a privately owned co-op. I'm paid to look after them in the off-season."

"Is there anyone else on the island now, Bob?"

"Not that I know of. Nobody here but me until April or May. If something happened to you, no one would know."

"I could have sworn I saw another light on the island last night," says Jack. "It wasn't your cabin either. It was down this side, on the south end."

Knifeblade Bob lowers his voice to a whisper. "I told you. Al-Qaeda could be here right now. Luckily we've got Corporal MacDonald to protect us."

Bob walks down to the far end of the cove, stops at a stylish West Coast vacation home. "This house is owned by a doctor from Vancouver. Guy named West."

"The doctor has good taste." Liz looks back to Bob. "Bob, can you show us where you found the foot?"

Knifeblade takes them down to the beach in the cove below the West house. A curving crescent of gravel and shells, bisected by a few boat docks.

"Here's where I found the foot."

They walk past a dock with a small boathouse surrounded by water on three sides. There is a distinctive totem pole at the end of the dock. Liz photographs it with her cell phone.

"What's in there, Bob?"

Bob makes a pot-smoking signal, gesturing to the boathouse. "My guess, hydroponics. BC's biggest cash crop."

Liz walks down the ramp to the shed and looks through the boards but can't see anything. The windowless boathouse is padlocked with a very solid lock.

"It's really dark in there. Any chance we can get inside?"

"Sorry, I don't have a key to it."

"Thanks Bob, you have been very helpful."

"I hope you Mounties catch the bastard."

Liz smiles. "We always get our man."

■ ■ ■

Back at Jack's cabin, Liz plops down in a broken-down recliner.

"Well, that was interesting, to say the least," she says.

"I don't think he's our guy." Jack is fixing sandwiches and coffee.

"He's quite the conspiracy theorist. Kind of a nutter, eh?"

"Bob's eccentric, but not crazy. He's not violent. Plus, he has a really nice yellow Lab."

"So?"

"Serial killers don't have dogs."

"Buffalo Bill did."

"That was a movie. The real guy they based that character on, Ed Gein, didn't have a dog. Besides, Bob lacks the charm, organization or guile of a psychopath."

"You're the expert."

"I am."

"I do think his obsession with knives is a bit odd."

"I wouldn't read too much into that. He's basically a hermit almost the entire year. He also quotes Shakespeare—that doesn't mean he wants to be a thespian. What we need is a body."

"What I need is a look inside that shed."

"Don't get off track here."

"If you were going to cut people up, wouldn't a windowless boathouse on a deserted island be a prime spot?"

"If I were going to cut people up, I wouldn't be stupid enough to allow their feet to float on shore," says Jack. "You still like Timmons for this?"

"Yes. Fouché found a picture of him fishing in front of something very similar. Look at this."

On her phone, Liz shows Jack the picture of the totem pole at the West boathouse and the picture of Timmons fishing, the same totem pole in the background.

"So what? You still don't have probable cause."

"Timmons has access to dart guns and tranquilizers. He likes runners. He is a rapist. I think he's escalating his serial sex crimes."

"Still conjecture. What do we *know*?"

Liz ticks off her points on her fingers. "Fourteen feet, twenty-two missing blondes, all in running shoes, dart gun. Timmons' victims were all blondes, all runners and he uses dart guns for work. It's Timmons."

"That's an *idée fixe*. You are too focused on Timmons. He attacked all of his victims in Stanley Park. Amanda was well outside that zone."

"Jack, if he is expanding to murder, he could be expanding his territory."

Jack argues, "These feet started showing up in 2007. That coincides with the rape timeline. How is that showing signs of escalation? Maybe he did escalate as you suggest and he did abduct Amanda, but that crime could have nothing to do with the severed feet."

Frustrated, Liz sighs. "I just have a feeling, Jack. He's the guy."

"Okay. I've been known to have hunches too. Let's work yours. Again, what do we know?"

"Timmons raped seven blond runners. Amanda was a blond runner."

"So let's start with blondes."

"Okay, Jack. Why blondes?"

"The blond gene was a mutation for survival. Paleolithic males chose blond mates because they stood out."

Liz says, "Well, in fairy tales, blondes suggest virginal beauty, sexuality. In actuality, only two percent of the world's population is blond."

"To wit, blondes are special. You might want to think about changing your hair color."

"Anything else?"

"Diana was a blonde."

"Princess Diana?"

"Yes, but I meant the Roman goddess, the huntress. She was also fleet of foot, a runner. These Diana figures are now the hunted. They have something the killer doesn't, so he's cutting off their feet."

"Assuming he has a classical education."

"Even if he doesn't, it's an elemental archetype, an atavistic response of a male hunter to a fair huntress."

"What? Track her down, rape and kill her?"

"Sure. Why not? If that's what floats your boat."

"Wow. I wouldn't want your worldview."

"No, you wouldn't."

"So, does he cut off the foot before or after he kills them?"

"Definitely before, what's the fun otherwise? He's punishing them."

"That's gruesome . . . Punishing them for what?"

"I don't know yet. Do you know how long any of the feet have been in the water?"

"No. Why?"

"It can help narrow things down."

"How?"

"It takes two weeks for a foot to naturally disarticulate, assuming it is weighed down."

"How do you know that?"

"Ever hear of the VENUS project?"

Jack goes to his laptop and types in: http://venus.uvic.ca/data/camera-stream/. Liz leans in, looking over his shoulder. She sees a time-lapse video of an animal carcass being eaten by crabs and sea scavengers. A bizarre underwater ballet in fast motion, dozens of shrimp and crabs scurrying over drifting flesh and bones. Vaguely horrifying.

"Just like on land, bodies decompose underwater in a predictable fashion. Forensic scientists at U-Vic ran experiments to see what happens to a submerged body."

"Don't tell me they used cadavers."

"No, pig carcasses at various depths. Scavengers nibbled away at the flesh."

Liz grimaces at the footage. The carcass looks very human.

Jack continues, "It took about two weeks for the pig's foot to disarticulate."

"So, if you have a foot that was in the water less than two weeks . . ."

"It's not natural disarticulation."

"And therefore either a crime or an unreported accident."

Liz looks at her watch. "Jesus, I have to get going. The last ferry leaves in an hour."

"I'll drop you off, unless you want to stay over . . ."

Pause. "Thanks, Jack." She smiles softly. "I don't think that's a good idea."

"Sorry, I didn't mean . . . I have a great couch."

"No, no. But thanks anyway. I—I have to get back."

17

Dawn again. After a dreamless sleep, thank God. Liz checks her watch. Her breath misting in the cool air. She clicks on her GPS watch and starts her run. Hard and fast into the trees. She begins to sweat despite the cold. She picks up the pace as she crosses over the footbridge and turns onto the side trail. She hears someone running behind her. She looks over her shoulder. A shadowy figure. She looks down and realizes that she's wearing nothing but her underwear, running barefoot in the fog-shrouded forest. *Wait . . . What . . . Let me sort this out . . .*

But she cannot wait. She runs faster, not knowing what direction to go. She hears footsteps behind her. The shrouded figure is chasing her through the trees. Panicking, she runs faster. The figure continues to chase her, pounding along, gaining. She leaps over logs and boulders—cutting her bare feet—the figure closes in—she runs into a bog, splashes through the mud—the steel cable, tight around her ankle—pulls her back and she falls flat—the figure is almost on her—she struggles with the cable but it's locked tight on her ankle—the figure descends on her with a huge meat cleaver, slamming it down. Liz screams.

She wakes with a start, drenched in sweat. She rubs her eyes and turns on a light. Four AM. *Shit. Never get back to sleep now.*

She looks at the end of the bed. A hooded figure looms over her, standing in the dark at the end of her bed. Liz gives a startled shout, fumbles in her drawer for a flashlight and pepper spray, knocking over the lamp. She grabs her cop's Kel-Lite, snaps the beam on, ready to bring the big, heavy cylinder down on the man's head but the figure is gone. Liz jumps up, grabs her cell phone, starts to dial 911, but hesitates, doesn't press send. She sweeps the light around the empty bedroom, moves into the hallway, moving from room to room with the pepper spray held absurdly out in front of her like a gun just as she'd been trained, wishing it *were* a gun, the absurdity of the RCMP's firearms regulations finally coming home to her. The beam of light dancing slightly, her hands shaking, breathing hard, clearing the house. It's empty . . . She's panting, drenched in sweat. She looks at her kitchen window. The curtain is blowing in the wind.

Shaken, she clears 911 from her cell and dials Fouché. "Doug, it's Liz. I'm sorry to be calling so late but I think someone was just in my house."

"I'll be right over. Do you want me to call a patrol car?"

"No. Just come over."

■ ■ ■

Liz opens the door for Fouché.

"Thanks for coming over. I know I should be able to handle it but this really threw me for a loop."

"Has it happened before?"

"Possibly. I've had some things moved in the house or a window was open and I thought I was just being absent-minded. Also, I think somebody has been following me on my runs. There are too many weird things happening."

"Any idea who it is?"

"Yeah. Who do you think?"

"Timmons? You don't know that it's him for sure, though."

"No, but come on. After our last encounter, he probably thinks I've ruined his life. I'm just his type—blond runner—so he's going to fuck with me and try to make me think I'm going crazy."

"We should call it in."

"No. Ward will take me off the case."

"You're already off the Stanley Park case. What do you want me to do?"

"I don't know. Play some cards? I can't go back to sleep and I don't want to be alone."

"Done. But tomorrow we get a tail on the guy or make sure a patrol car drives by your place. I won't say anything to Ward or Richards."

Liz pulls out a deck of cards and expertly shuffles them.

"Fine. I don't know how you'll explain a patrol car driving by my place without telling them. But for now, the game is rummy. Aces high or low. Loser buys bagels."

■ ■ ■

Exhausted, Liz slowly drives through the winding roads of the Endowment Lands of the University of British Columbia's campus. She's wearing a slightly rumpled uniform blouse, hair tousled as usual. She sees students walking to their early morning classes, shouldering heavy backpacks. Most of them blissfully unaware of the problems that pervade outside their cloistered campus. She parks and heads into the college coffeehouse to meet two of Amanda's friends, who sadly are now very much aware that bad things can happen to good people.

She walks up to the table and introduces herself to the two young women.

"Hello, I'm Corporal Liz MacDonald with the RCMP." Flashes her ID.

The first girl holds out her hand. "I'm Meaghan Donnelly."

The other girl nods and says, "And I'm Julie Stevens."

"Thank you so much for meeting with me." Liz pulls out her notebook. "I just have a few questions. Is there anything that stands out about the night of the party?"

"No. Everyone was having a great time. We had a cookout at the beach. Listened to some music."

"Yeah. She and Caleb were celebrating their engagement. He had proposed on their two-year anniversary. So we planned a little party for them."

"She was so excited about it. She told us we were both going to be her maids of honor." Julie chokes up.

"We might still be." Meaghan says quietly. "We're going to find her."

Liz redirects. "What time did she leave?"

"I think around midnight. Caleb left about an hour later."

"Yeah, he came running back to the beach, super-upset. He said her SUV was up there with the engine running, no Amanda."

"And Caleb didn't walk her back to her car?"

"No."

"Why not?"

"Ah, I don't know. She had to leave and he wanted to party on, I guess."

"Did Caleb leave the party at any point?"

"No. Definitely not."

"We looked all over the woods and didn't see anything," says Meaghan. "We were all calling for her. But I knew something bad happened."

"Yes. Amanda doesn't even drink," says Julie. "She doesn't smoke pot. She is very precise about things. She wouldn't just leave her car running like that."

"What about another boyfriend? Someone on the side maybe?"

"No way."

"Yup. She was faithful."

Liz refers to her notes. "We spoke with Caleb. He said that Amanda had dated another guy a few years ago. Do you know any of her exes?"

"We never met the guy. She only dated him for a couple of months."

"Do you know his name?"

Julie shakes her head. "I can't remember."

"You can't remember because she never told us," says Meaghan. "She called him 'Mr. Big' like *Sex in the City*."

"Why did she call him Mr. Big?"

"Amanda loved *Sex in the City*. She said he reminded her of the guy on the show that Carrie dated, because he would run so hot and cold."

"But she never referred to him by his real name? You didn't find that odd?"

Meaghan glances at Julie. "Of course we did. Especially since he wouldn't let her hang out with us."

"Yeah. He was weird. Apparently refused to get his picture taken. Who does that?"

"I don't know. Did Amanda ever confide to you that she thought she was being stalked?"

"She was."

"By Mr. Big?"

"Probably."

"How do you know that?"

"One time we carpooled to a track meet," says Julie. "Afterwards, her car had been broken into. Amanda was really thrown for a loop. Nothing was missing."

"So what makes you think it was her stalker?"

"He left a note. It said, 'Great track meet Amanda. I miss you.' She started shaking and crying."

"She was scared," adds Meaghan.

"Scared of Mr. Big? Did he threaten her, or abuse her in any way?"

"Not that we know of. But her cat went missing. She was convinced Mr. Big did it."

"Did she report this? Did she try to get a restraining order?"

"No. She was afraid it would escalate the situation," says Julie. "She ended up moving back home with her parents from campus housing. She thought that would be safer."

"You don't have any photos? Ever see any photos of the ex?"

"Sorry, no. We told you, he didn't let people photograph him." Meaghan shakes her head.

"We can give you a list of the other girls on the team if you want to ask them. You never know. Someone may have met the guy."

Liz pulls out a photo of Timmons and shows it to the girls.

"Have you ever seen this man?"

"Oh, yeah," says Meaghan. "Is that the guy that was arrested for the Stanley Park rapes?"

"It is."

"No, we've never seen him in person, except on TV. After those rapes all started, we never ran alone at Stanley Park. Strict buddy system."

"Good. That's smart."

"If he *was* the ex, we'd have no way of knowing."

"Okay. Thanks for your help, ladies. If anything else springs to mind, please call me." Liz hands them both a card.

"She's dead, isn't she?" Meaghan looks at Liz earnestly.

The directness of the question catches Liz off guard. She clears her throat. "Let's hope not."

Julie interjects with a wan smile, "Hope means you entertain illusions."

"Jean Paul Sartre?"

"Henry Miller. I'm a Lit major. Sorry. This whole thing has really . . ." Julie trails off.

"I know. I'm sorry, but I know." Liz thanks the girls again and leaves.

As Liz heads to her car, the beauty of the campus strikes her. A shaft of light glimmering through the delicate branches of a tree, creating long, dark shadows on the ground. *It's funny how trees can either look beautiful or ominous depending on how you look at them.* Liz thinks. *Beauty coexists with despair.* She shivers. Julie was right; hope does mean you entertain illusions.

18

The next morning at 10:00 AM, Liz, Richards and Fouché listen on the speakerphone in the conference room.

"Liz. It's Zach. Your DNA results are in. You're not going to like this: Foot fourteen belongs to Amanda Ferguson."

"Are you sure?"

"It's a 99.9% match."

"Okay. Thanks." Liz hangs up. "Goddammit! I was hoping we'd find her alive."

Fouché puts his hand on her shoulder. "Liz. It's tragic news for Amanda's family. But it's the first time we've been able to link a missing person with a foot. It proves your theory."

Richards looks over his notes. "I'll follow up on the list the girls gave Liz. One of Amanda's teammates said she thinks she met the mystery boyfriend. I'm going to take the file of usual suspects plus Timmons to see if she recognizes anyone."

Ward leans into the doorway.

"Hold your horses. We just got a tip. My office. Now."

■ ■ ■

On her desktop computer Ward plays a 911 call recording.

An electronic beep, then a somewhat tinny voice answers.

"9-1-1—What's your emergency?"

"Amanda Ferguson. That poor girl! I saw her—she, she jumped! Off the New Westminster bridge. About 2:00 AM on Saturday night. It was horrible!"

"Sir? Were you able to identify—how do you know it was her?"

"Her picture is all over the papers. She was wearing cutoff shorts and some kind of track jacket." The man's voice cracks with emotion. *"She hit the water awful hard. That fall would have killed anyone."*

"What is your name sir?"

"She was so young . . ." The line goes dead.

"Sir? Sir?"

Ward stops the recording. "Suicide."

Liz interjects, "Based on an anonymous tip? Why did he wait so long to call it in? He could be the killer for all we know."

Fouché agrees. "Or it could be a hoax."

Ward counters, "The man sounded distressed. I don't think it was a hoax."

"Inspector Ward, with all due respect, Amanda's texts, social media, engagement all indicate a happy girl with plans. Not someone who is going to kill herself."

Richards isn't buying it. "How did she even get to the bridge?"

"It's not that far from where her truck was found."

Richards says, "It's *twelve* miles. On foot. No pun intended."

Liz agrees. "That's a two-hour run, four-hour walk. And if it was suicide, how did her foot disarticulate so quickly? It takes two weeks underwater and Amanda has only been missing for seventy-two hours. And that's assuming the body was weighed down."

"How do we know that?" says Ward.

"U-Vic has an underwater body farm. Their experiment shows that it takes two weeks for a foot to disarticulate."

"Sounds dodgy to me."

"Maybe her foot dislocated on impact or she hit part of the bridge on her way down," says Fouché.

Exasperated, Liz says, "Where's the body? Where are all the bodies? Inspector Ward, why do you refuse to see what is happening here?"

"It was suicide, Liz. Why are you grasping at straws?"

"Because no one else is! It is our job to protect and uphold the law. *Mantiens le droit!* And this one is just not right."

"Don't lecture me Corporal—"

"There is a family out there with a dead daughter, sister and fiancée. They deserve the truth."

Ward looks at her but has no reply.

Liz softens. "I'm sorry. Look, there must be CCTV footage for the bridge. Before we notify the family, at least let me speed through it. Give me twenty-four hours. Please."

"You've got twelve. Then we have a press conference. We need to close this case."

Ward leaves. Liz watches her go.

■ ■ ■

The killer logs on to Rosie's website and reads with amusement:

The Missing-Missing are a voiceless group. They may not even have a missing person's report filed when they disappear. To authorities, they are just another nutjob or hooker or drug addict or whatever other categories they deem unworthy of their attention. What of my list of missing twenty-two women? Are they missing or Missing-Missing? Does it matter, really? They are gone and no one is looking for answers. Too many mothers are missing their children. These twenty-two girls have no ties to gangs, crime, drugs or anything seemingly dangerous. They are all blond and all runners. They all have disappeared from the Lower Mainland, leaving no clues as to what happened. But to me, that says a lot. It says there is a serial killer stalking young blond runners. And we have severed human feet washing ashore all over the Lower Mainland and the Gulf Islands. Why aren't DNA tests being run on these feet to match them to these missing girls? Doesn't the RCMP want to know what happened? What is it going to take? One of the commanding officer's daughters to disappear to get a task force on this? Something is rotten in the state of Denmark.

Too bad Rosie isn't a blonde, he thinks. But perhaps he could make an exception. Some of her crackpot theories hit too close to home for his taste. Next, he logs on to a website: easytospy.com. Breaking into Liz's car and installing a spyware app on Liz's phone was the simplest and easiest thing he could do to keep an eye on Liz and the investigation. Takes the legwork out of stalking. The app shows Liz's precise location. Next he checks her text messages.

Jack—DNA confirms foot belongs to Amanda. Ward says it's a suicide.

Liz, that doesn't make sense.

I know. Call in a bit, researching CCTV footage to disprove theory.

He cheerfully logs off his computer and prepares for today's task at hand.

19

Jack, his hand shaking, pours himself another stiff drink. He looks at his maps and charts where he has been charting the locations of the feet. Classical music plays on his iPod. His map is fraught with Jack's shaky scrawl and hand-drawn arrows regarding spring and full-moon tides, red pins representing where the feet have been discovered, green pins representing where girls have gone missing. Stymied, he stares at the wall. Nothing comes to him. Nothing. *Are they floating down the Fraser River? Are they floating up from the Gulf? How could it be possible to float upriver? Tick, tock*. He knows it's just a matter of time before he is adding yet another pin to this wall. *Tick, tock*. If he could have figured this out sooner, would Amanda have disappeared? *Tick, tock*.

Enraged, Jack picks up his Scotch bottle and throws it against the charts and maps. The bottle breaks, liquor pouring down the wall.

"Fuck . . . Fuck! Fuck!"

Spent, Jack looks at his chart, whiskey slowly dripping down, making the ink spider out. He grabs a towel to blot it when he spots something. *Wait.* There are three gaps, or "passes" which funnel the tide into—*and out of*—the Gulf Islands: Active, Porlier and Gabriola. Porlier Pass is only a few miles from his own island, directly across from the mouth of the Fraser River. He picks up a copy of the Tidal Current Tables, a large paperback book filled with row after row of numbers and figures in neat little columns, a useful piece of obsoledia in this digital age. He looks up the tides and currents for the night of Amanda's disappearance. Spring tides—the larger range of tides that happen every two weeks. Jack draws arrows on his chart, vectors showing the strength and direction of the current and prevailing westerly winds. With another color, he draws arrows from the locations of every foot back to the river. Looks outside at the waning full moon. Looks back at his charts. The arrows match.

■ ■ ■

Liz, bleary-eyed, is speeding through CCTV footage at her desk. She has been scanning the footage for the past four hours. Even at four times the speed, it will take forever. Not one pedestrian, very few cars and no Amanda. Liz sticks with it, drinking coffee. She watches the footage as the sun rises with unnatural swiftness over the bridge. Still no Amanda. Liz's mobile rings.

"Corporal MacDonald."

"You and I both know Amanda didn't jump off a bridge."

"Rosie?"

"Yeah."

"Your source tell you that? Rosie, I'm checking the New Westminster Bridge's CCTV cameras as we speak."

"Yeah, well, check your e-mail."

"What? Why?"

Rosie hangs up. Liz hesitates, clicks on her inbox. She opens an e-mail from Rosie that contains a forwarded e-mail with the subject line, "Watch Me" and a link. Liz clicks on the link. Liz's hand goes to her mouth, shocked. The killer's video plays before her eyes. Delibes' *Lakmé* emanating from her computer. Nude Amanda tied to a steel table, pleading with an unseen figure.

"Please, please . . ."

"Scream all you want . . . It's just the two of us."

Liz stops the video and picks up her phone. "Inspector Ward, Liz MacDonald. I am sorry to call so late. But I think you might want to get down here right away."

■ ■ ■

Liz, Ward, Richards and Fouché are clustered around Liz's computer screen watching the killer's video. The disembodied screaming echoes from the tiny speaker. Sets your teeth on edge.

Richards presses stop. "I'm going to be sick."

Fouché can't even look at the screen.

Ward composes herself. "Oh Christ . . . Where did that come from?"

"Rosie George e-mailed it to me. It was sent to her anonymously from a one-time e-mail address with an untraceable server somewhere in Pakistan. Complete dead end."

"Can this go live?"

"God, I hope not."

Fouché interjects, "Only if the killer wants it to."

Ward says, "Get this to our IT forensic team. Maybe they can find something."

Fouché nods. "I already called them in."

Liz points to the video. "This looks like water reflecting. Could be a boathouse or some type of structure near the water. We need to pump up ambient noise to try to pinpoint a location."

Richards adds, "Maybe we could get a voiceprint of the killer's voice."

"It's probably too distorted, but I'll try." Fouché goes to his computer.

Ward looks to the three. "Look. We screwed up on this. I screwed up. Now we know . . . Let's proceed accordingly. Richards, bring Timmons in for questioning."

"On what charge?"

"Double parking."

■ ■ ■

Richards, Fouché and several constables surround Timmons' house. Flashlights search the premises, beaming in through the windows, radios squawking softly. Fouché bangs hard and loud on the door.

"RCMP! Timmons! Open up! We've got a warrant!"

There is no response. Richards signals the constables to knock down the door on three. They break in the door with a battering ram. Mail and newspapers piled up in the hallway below the mail slot. They flash their lights, clearing each room. The house is deserted. Richards gets Ward on his cell phone.

"He's not here. Looks like he hasn't been here for a while."

"Damn. Better bring in Rosie George, just for questioning about the e-mail. Maybe she knows where it came from."

"Do we get a warrant?"

"No . . . Just voluntary, assisting us with our inquires, etc. *And* her computer, do you copy?"

"Rosie and her computer. Roger that."

■ ■ ■

Rosie is seated at the interrogation table. Her arms are crossed as she glares at the two-way mirror. She lights a cigarette, flips them the bird, knowing "they" are behind it. Liz takes a deep breath and enters the room.

"Rosie. Sorry, but you can't smoke in here."

"Oh, sorry." She takes another drag, hardly glancing up, makes no move to put it out. "As usual, civil liberties go out the window with you people."

"Rosie . . ."

"You have constables banging down my door. They steal my computer. They toss my apartment. No warrant. Nothing!"

"There is a lot at stake here. I'm sorry if that was mishandled. I know you only sent us the video to help but we need to see if there is a way of tracing the video back to the killer."

"Try asking. 'Ms. George, may we please take a look at your computer.' It's amazing what manners will do."

"Again, I'm sorry. But I have a few questions for you about the video. What time did you receive it?"

"Minutes before I called you and forwarded it to you. You could have known that by looking at the e-mail chain."

"Have you ever had any correspondence with the email address, ah, 'runners4me@pk.com' before?"

"No."

"Have you ever been approached by a perpetrator before?"

"Possibly. I get all kinds of nuts e-mailing me. Usually it is just families who need to be heard but there are sickos out there trying to get their rocks off."

"Any of them legitimate?"

"I don't think so but who's to say? I've never been approached personally. No Deep Throat calls or anything like that. You have my computer. You can check it out for yourself. I'm sure you've already discovered it's from a blind server."

"We did. Why do you think the killer sent you the video?"

"Because he wanted the word out. Anyone who reads my blog knows I despise the RCMP. The killer assumed the last thing I'd do is forward it to you. He thought I would post it. Which I'd never do. Even victims need their dignity. But you promised, Liz. You looked me in the eye and gave me your word you would solve this case."

"I did. And I still mean it. From one East Van girl to another, Rosie . . ." *If only it were that easy*, Liz thinks. *Tick, tock.*

"Are we done here?"

"Sorry, let me check with Inspector Ward. In the mean time I can get you a cup of coffee or a snack . . ."

Rosie rolls her eyes. "Skip the snack, get me another pack of cigarettes. And a coffee, light and sweet . . . like me."

■ ■ ■

In the conference room twenty minutes later, Liz and Fouché are poring over files, exhausted. Richards enters.

"We just sent Rosie home. Can't wait to see her next blog on the RCMP. I don't think we'll be getting a favorable review."

Liz looks up. "Can you blame her?"

Richards asks Fouché, "Anything from IT on the e-mail?"

"Untraceable. Complete dead end."

"What about Rosie's computer?"

"Nothing yet."

Frustrated, Liz reacts, "There has to be something! Can we track him based on the brand of stainless steel table?"

"Liz, we're not going to find him that way," says Fouché.

"What about credit cards, phone? Any luck with property records?"

"Not yet."

"Let's narrow it down to Francisco Island, there can't be more than a dozen houses. See if there has been an unreported inheritance or new sale. Maybe we'll get lucky."

Liz's cell phone rings and she answers it. "MacDonald."

"Liz? It's Jack. Oh good, you're up. I have something."

"Me too. You first."

Liz exits the conference room with her phone. Fouché gives her a look. She waves him off.

"We've been looking at it backwards," says Jack. "The feet aren't floating *down* the Fraser, they are drifting *up* from the Gulf Islands on the flood tide."

"So our killer operates from the Gulf Islands?"

"Probably. Maybe. What's your news?"

"I can't talk about it right now. Can you meet me this afternoon?"

"I'll pick you up at the ferry."

"No, I'll just grab a water taxi. Keep working."

Liz hangs up and turns. Fouché is standing there in the doorway.

"Who are you meeting with, Liz?"

"None of your business."

"Well, Liz, it is my business if you are investigating our case. You're going to see Jack Harris."

"How do you know that?"

"It doesn't take a detective."

"I'm sorry, but I want to talk to Jack one more time and I want a look in that boathouse."

"Is that wise? You have no probable cause here. You can't go poking around somebody's boathouse without calling me first. It's not safe. It's against procedure."

"I think it's the next logical step. I'll call you if I see anything suspicious."

"Okay, it's your funeral. I'll have my mobile on."

Liz walks away, leaving Fouché in the doorway.

■ ■ ■

Long Harbour ferry dock. Empty, windswept, cold. No one to meet her, so Liz, out of uniform but feeling conspicuous in a bright yellow rain jacket, hikes down to the B&B, calls a water taxi and orders a latte. The small covered speedboat arrives minutes later, picks her up, sets out across the smooth gray water for Jack's island. The water taxi driver, an ancient in a faded gray sweater, cigarette dangling from his mouth, is not in a talkative mood. Which suits Liz fine. Eventually, they slow and come-to at Jack's dock. The lights are off. Door's open. No sign of life. She pays off the water taxi driver and walks up the dock toward the empty doorway.

"Jack?" No answer.

Liz enters the cabin and steps on a piece of glass from the broken whiskey bottle. Jack is hung-over, lying in a heap on the couch, hand trembling, a crude bandage made from a dishrag tied around it.

"Must've been some party," says Liz.

"Maid's day off."

Briskly, Liz pushes debris on his table aside and pulls out her laptop. "Take a look at this."

She plays the video. The music, and the screaming finally stop. Jack has no reaction to the horror before him.

"Play it back . . . Again."

"Seriously?"

"Yes . . . Stop. Go back . . ."

"How can you keep watching this?"

"I'm not, I'm listening. Play it back again. Stop. Did you hear that?"

Liz plays the video again. A low discordant tone bleeds through the music.

"That's not part of the music . . . that's a foghorn. I can't be positive but it sounds like Virago Point, in Porlier Pass, on the end of Galiano."

"How on earth do you know that?"

"Foghorns have specific identification signatures. Virago is two long and one short."

"I thought the Coast Guard discontinued fog signals a while ago."

"True. But there was such an outcry they reinstated a few of them."

Liz sits up. "So the boathouse has to be near Virago."

Jack looks at her. "Liz, Virago Point is only a few miles from here."

"I need a look in that boathouse."

"What boathouse?"

"You know which boathouse."

"There have to be hundreds of boathouses in range of that foghorn. We have no reason to make some unknown doctor with a summer home a suspect just because he has a boathouse."

"On an island where a foot was found. And across the bay from where another foot was found. And he's a doctor."

"What else do we have?"

"Timmons."

"No proof. No connection. No forensic evidence. Just a profile."

"Not so fast. He has no alibi for the night of Amanda's disappearance. He has easy access to animal tranquilizers. And we have a picture of him fishing on the Gulf Islands in front of a boathouse with the same damn totem pole. And he's done a runner."

"*I* fish in the Gulf Islands. Totem poles like that one are a dime a dozen up here. I'm not even positive that is Virago Point's foghorn. And he could have taken a weekend trip. All circumstantial. Look, I need a drink. Want one?"

Liz looks at his shaking hand.

"I'll stick with coffee. But you better have one, I wouldn't want you having a seizure."

■ ■ ■

In Conference Room B, Fouché scrolls through a property records website, stops suddenly on a deed for property on Francisco Island. The former owner of record is Dr. Ralph West. With a quitclaim deed to a new owner: William Timmons.

"Holy shit . . ."

Fouché dials Liz's mobile phone, which goes to voice mail. *Shit.*

"Liz . . . It's Doug. Timmons owns the boathouse! There was a quitclaim deed from his stepdad, Dr. Ralph West. Don't go to that boathouse without me. I'll be there as soon as I can. I'll take the next ferry."

Fouché gets up and rushes out.

20

Knifeblade Bob is sharpening his knife. Playing John Coltrane's "My Favorite Things" on his iPod. He languidly caresses the smooth blade, feeling it rasp satisfyingly against the grain of the whetstone, gliding through the oil. Daisy perks up her head, her floppy ears lifting a bit, lets out a low growl, and then barks. Again, louder. Bob listens.

"Did you scare up another bear, girl? You stay inside."

He takes a flashlight, his stainless bridge cable knife, and some bear spray, walks outside, smiling in the knowledge that he is, literally, loaded for bear.

■ ■ ■

It's late. Liz and Jack have been working through the night. They have polished off a plate of sandwiches, a pot of coffee and half a bottle of Macallan. Maps, files and paperwork are skewed all over his kitchen table. Jack watches Liz sip her coffee.

"So I'm guessing your dad is the reason you don't drink," he says.

"Don't want to roll genetic dice, so to speak."

"I suspect there is more to it than that."

Liz hesitates. "My father used to come home drunk. If he was whistling, it meant he'd won at the racetrack. If he wasn't, it meant the belt. He'd find any excuse and after a while he didn't need one at all. He'd pull the belt off slowly and fold it into a loop. He'd raise his arm high above his head and then—" Liz slams her hand on the table.

"I'm sorry. Is that why you run?"

"It's the only time I don't have to think."

"Did your father . . . ?"

"Not that it's your business . . . But no. The beating was enough. I run to numb my memory. Is that why you drink?"

"Pretty much."

"What else?"

Jack stands, crosses to the window. Looks out across the bay.

He continues, "I've seen *unspeakable* things. Things done to young girls, to women, to children. By men, basically. The mistake people make is calling these guys monsters. Because they aren't some mythological bogeyman lurking in the shadows. They walk among us. They're real. They're your neighbor. The guy bagging your groceries. The kindly old guy who helps you change your tire on the side of the road with a young girl bound and gagged in the trunk of his car. I drink so I don't keep seeing these things on a perpetual loop in my head. I drink because I can't stop them all."

Liz looks at him for a long moment. "Well. We're going to stop this one."

She taps her finger on a photograph of Knifeblade Bob's island.

"I'm going to look inside that boathouse."

"You'll never get a warrant."

"Who said anything about a warrant? I just want a look."

"*You* can't go, you'd compromise the evidence chain."

Liz looks at Jack. "Don't even think about it. You'd get arrested for breaking and entering."

"If I got caught. And how would I get caught?"

"I would arrest you," says Liz.

"For what?"

"Drunk and disorderly. You're half in the bag as it is."

"You wouldn't arrest me."

Liz takes handcuffs out of her purse. "I would and I'd handcuff you too . . . for your own protection."

"Do you always carry handcuffs?"

"I never know when I might need them."

"Do you even know how to use them?"

"Yes, of course I do."

Jack moves closer and takes her handcuffs.

"Really? Do you know how to get out of them?"

"Yes . . ."

Jack steps behind her, closer, his breath on her neck.

"What if you were overpowered? Restrained by a suspect with your own cuffs?"

"Depends on the situation. Am I in the trunk of a car, or just in a room?"

"In a cabin. Somewhere in the Gulf Islands."

Jack speed-cuffs her, arms behind her.

"Come on, Jack. Not funny."

Jack leans closer and whispers in her ear, "A serial killer has captured you. You have one minute before he comes back."

Liz is uncomfortable.

"Only a minute?"

"That's all you get. One minute to live. Tick, tock."

Jack crosses back to his recliner and sits down, smiles. Liz does something behind her back, undoes the cuffs and spins them around her finger.

"How did you do that so fast?"

"I taught a kidnap, escape and evasion class for women." She holds up a handcuff key. "Also, I have a key in my back pocket."

"You cheated."

"Really?"

Liz moves to where Jack is sitting, straddles him, sits facing him on his lap, gently, seductively pushing him back into his chair.

Whispering in his ear, "All's fair in love and war, they say."

She kisses him softly on the lips.

Jack looks at her. "Really. Is this love?"

"No." She gently bites his lip. "An intervention."

She speed-cuffs him to the wooden chair arm and then deposits the handcuff key on the desk, just out of his reach. "You've been captured by a serial killer. You have one minute to live. Tick, tock."

"This isn't funny, Liz."

"It is a little bit." She dumps the Macallan in the sink, grabs one of Jack's flashlights, and heads to the door.

Jack struggles to reach for a broom handle to knock the key off. He can't quite reach it. Liz grabs Jack's boat keys on a yellow float from a hook by the door.

"Liz! Where the hell are you going?"

"Where do you think? I'll be back in half an hour. You should be able to gnaw through your chair by then."

"Liz, uncuff me and I'll go with you."

Liz shakes her head. "Uh-uh. Sorry."

"At least tell me you're armed."

"This isn't the Wild West, cowboy. I'm off-duty. We don't carry off-duty weapons in Canada. Bye."

"Liz! Goddamn it!"

She exits the cabin.

■ ■ ■

Knifeblade Bob walks through the forest toward the West house, at the far end of the cove, shining his light around. If it is a bear, he doesn't want to startle it and make the bear defensive.

In a loud, assertive voice, he calls, "Hey, bear! Hey, bear, bear, bear! . . ."

Bob reaches the West house and shines the light toward the window. It's empty. He walks around the house. He spots a light down by the beach.

"Fucking Al-Qaeda! Not on my watch." He heads down to the shoreline.

■ ■ ■

Liz walks down to the dock. She stops. She can clearly hear Daisy barking, the sound echoing across the bay from Bob's cabin. His light is still on. Liz gets into Jack's tinner, starts the outboard with the key. Her phone vibrates. She grabs it and checks her voice mail, which fades in and out.

"Liz. It's —immons owns — a quitclaim from — West. Don't — house with— be there as—"

The line goes dead. Liz tries to call him back. No reception. She casts off, hits the throttle and powers over the black water toward Francisco Island and Knifeblade's light.

■ ■ ■

Jack, handcuffed to his recliner, hears Daisy barking incessantly from across the water. He struggles to break free, still drunk.

"Fuck!"

Frantically, he manhandles the entire heavy awkward chair and smashes the arm of the chair against the wall, breaking it free. He stands up and gets the key, uncuffs his wrist. He heads across the room. By his bed, he kneels down and pulls up a floorboard, revealing a small Smith & Wesson AirLite .357 Magnum revolver in an ankle holster. He grabs the pistol, snaps open the cylinder, checks it for ammo, straps it to his ankle, and replaces the board.

He runs down to his dock but his tinner is gone.

"Shit."

He grabs his kayak and paddle, drags it down from the dock to the beach, stumbles as he climbs in—almost capsizing—and paddles over the slick water toward Francisco Island.

■ ■ ■

Liz lands the tinner on Bob's beach. She hears Daisy, still barking up at Bob's house, heads up the beach to the cabin, flashlight in hand.

"Bob?" She moves onto the porch. Daisy barking frantically. "Bob! It's Liz MacDonald, RCMP! Are you all right?"

No response. She edges around the door, her back to the wall, takes a quick peek through the window. Daisy is jumping and scratching at the door, barking. The one-room cabin is empty aside from the dog. She decides to leave her there, runs down the steps and onto the forest trail leading into the interior of the island.

Liz moves swiftly through the tall, dark timber, past the wolf sign, hikes along the path to the West place and down to the boathouse. She shuts off the flashlight. Walks out on the short dock, the boards groaning underfoot. The door of the shed is ajar, a dim light shines from within. She hesitates, pivots around and swiftly looks inside, pulling her head back an instant later.

Then she turns on her flashlight and walks inside. The boathouse is deserted, but packed with hydroponic equipment. Pot is growing everywhere, water irrigation systems drip, grow lights glow dully, bags of fertilizer stacked in the corner. An old cedar-strip canoe in the rafters. Maybe Knifeblade Bob wasn't such a nut after all, at least not about the pot growing.

Suddenly a board creaks—she turns just as something drops over her head—she gags and drops her flashlight, struggling against the thing choking her, hands windmilling wildly behind and around her at empty air—no breath—trying to find what it is that has grabbed her. Liz has an animal control noose around her neck. Timmons is on the end of the long pole. She flops around, fighting a reverse tug of war.

"If you're wondering what the fuck has grabbed you, it's called a Ketch-All. Very useful in my line of work."

She croaks out, "Timmons, you fucking bastard!"

"The more you struggle, the quicker you pass out."

Timmons tightens the noose with a ratcheting sound. Liz tries to hold her breath—but eventually of course she has to let it out and the next one just won't come. The darkness comes and Liz loses consciousness.

21

Liz wakes up in her underwear—cotton panties and thin camisole—hands and feet secured with zip ties. She's hanging by her zip-tied hands from a hook on a manual chain hoist secured to a beam above, incredibly vulnerable. Unspeakably painful. Her hands going numb, her rotator cuffs burning. She can just keep most of her weight off the plastic zip ties already cutting into her hands by standing on tiptoe—but she can only do that so long before her feet collapse and the full weight comes onto her hands, which are starting to bleed.

Timmons sits quietly in the shadows of the boathouse, smoking a cigarette, watching Liz. The end of his cigarette glows orange as he inhales.

"Feeling a little sore? I often wonder what a dog feels after the noose. How *does* it feel?"

"Fuck you Tim—"

He stands and raises the chain hoist a few ratcheting links, raising Liz off the floor.

She screams. Catches her breath. "What did you do to those girls?"

"I gave them what they needed. What they deserved."

Calmly, slowly, sensually, Timmons puts on a pair of surgical gloves.

Liz hoarsely asks, "Why? What did they ever do to you? Are you that far gone?"

Timmons moves close to her until he is inches from her lips.

"You're about to find out." He whispers in her ear, "I'll be right back, don't go anywhere. Too bad I can't just love you and let you go."

"Fuck you, you fuck—"

Suddenly, Timmons duct-tapes Liz's mouth. Gives her cheek a loving caress. Timmons exits the boathouse. Liz looks desperately around for a means of escape. A tool. Anything. Nothing she can reach.

■ ■ ■

Jack paddles hard across the smooth black water, slams the kayak up onto the gravel beach in front of Bob's place, steps out with his gun in hand. It is pitch-black. The kind of black and quiet that is either completely peaceful or completely terrifying. He hesitates, sees the light in Bob's cabin, hears Daisy barking and heads toward the cabin.

"Bob? Liz?"

He looks quickly in the window, sees Daisy going berserk but the room is empty. Bob is nowhere to be seen. Jack turns and follows the forest trail toward the cove, down to the other end of the island.

■ ■ ■

Knifeblade Bob, flashlight in hand, having traversed the whole of his island without encountering a single bear, wolf, or Al-Qaeda operative, comes out of the trees onto the crunching gravel of the beach near the West house. A strange tinner is pulled up on shore in the cove, not far from the boathouse, water lapping against the side.

"What the hell?"

He shines the light on the boat. There is a blue plastic tarp covering it. He lifts the tarp, stops cold, his face dissolving in shock, horrified by what he sees, gagging, stumbling backwards. Staring lifelessly back at him in the beam of his flashlight is a tall blond girl, nude, wrapped in clear Visqueen, stone-cold dead. And missing a foot, the bloody stump protruding grotesquely from the plastic.

Bob screams, drops the light, back-pedaling. He turns—and suddenly he gets hit with something small and sharp in his shoulder. He pulls it out, incredulous, sees what it is—*yes, that's a dart.*

There is a figure before him. A man in a hoodie. Swaying, Bob fumbles for his knife. He tries to throw it at his assailant but runs out of steam and collapses to the ground. The knife lands in a driftwood stump, point first. With a surgical-gloved hand, the man in the hoodie pulls the knife out of the stump. He hesitates for a moment, looking at the extraordinary knife, which seems to have been hammered out of steel cable, then tucks it into his belt. He drags Knifeblade Bob to the boat, dumps him in and covers him with the Visqueen and then the blue tarp. Next to the nude, pale, lifeless body of Amanda.

■ ■ ■

At the cost of excruciating pain, Liz swings her feet back and forth and finally gets a purchase with her legs and bare feet on the chain dangling from the chain hoist. She manages to crank it down a couple of links, giving her just enough slack to slip her zip-tied hands off the hook—she crashes instantly to the floor, knocking the wind out of her momentarily.

She grunts, sits up, sucking air. She rips the duct-tape from her mouth and, with her teeth, *tightens* the zip ties on her wrists. She takes a deep breath and, spreading her elbows apart, in one fluid motion, slams her wrists into her stomach. The pressure pops the zip tie free, her bloody cuts screaming pain.

Ignoring it, she works on freeing her feet. She takes off her braided paracord bracelet and unfurls the paracord. Threading the cord through the zip ties on her feet, she makes two knots and a loop on either end to form a friction saw and quickly pulls the cord back and forth to cut the zip tie. The paracord melts through the plastic and makes short work of it.

Free, Liz looks outside the open door. From a distance she sees Timmons' flashlight bobbing down the beach trail. She looks frantically around for a weapon—no luck.

■ ■ ■

Timmons walks down the dock to his boathouse, carrying a canvas tool bag. As he opens the door, he says, "I have something *special* for you, sweetheart."

He walks in to find Liz gone and the shed empty.

"What the fuck!"

There is literally nowhere for her to hide. The only way out would have been the path up to the house or down to the beach. Either direction, he would have spotted her. Timmons desperately removes the tarp covering a work-bench. Nothing.

"Fuck!"

Timmons exits, slamming the door behind him.

■ ■ ■

Shivering from the shockingly cold water, Liz gasps as she surfaces from underwater beneath the dock. Overhead, Liz can hear Timmons' feet running on the dock's planks and she can feel them vibrate. She waits until Timmons is gone, climbs out of the water onto the dock, catches her breath and runs down the dock toward shore.

Liz sprints down to the beach, stretches out barefoot on the rough stone shingle. Timmons, half way up the trail to his house, turns and sees her running, silhouetted against the water. Timmons throws down the bag and chases her down the beach. Liz runs, feet bloodied by the mussel shells. Throwing a glance over her shoulder, she sees Timmons following and loops away from the beach's barnacle-encrusted rocks, vaults the drift wood logs at the end of the beach, and runs up into the woods. Timmons follows.

■ ■ ■

Jack moves quietly, approaches the West house, heads for the dock and the now-deserted boathouse. He draws his gun and enters the boathouse. He sees the chain hoist, the broken zip ties, and Liz's clothes in a pile. "Shit!"

He exits the shed and looks to see where they might have gone. No sign of anyone—the beach below is empty. He heads back up the hill toward Timmons' house, which now has a light on.

■ ■ ■

Timmons chases her through the trees. She runs faster, leaping over logs and boulders. Timmons is closing on her now—her wounded feet slowing her—running slightly uphill, sucking in air, feet flying, relying on her runner's stamina to stay just ahead of him—but suddenly, at the top of the hill, she stops short, skidding, balancing precariously on the edge of a cliff, sixty or seventy feet above the water.

Timmons stops a short distance from the edge. Winded, he approaches her slowly.

"Damn! You are fast. Let me catch my breath . . ." He smiles. "Oh that's right, nowhere to go, girlie. Did you forget we were on an island?"

Liz gasps for breath, teetering on the edge. Trapped.

Timmons straightens. "Ready to go another round, sweetheart?"

"Fuck you."

She turns and jumps over the edge of the cliff, down into the water below with a yell.

22

From the front porch of the West house, Jack hears Liz yell, echoing through the trees and across the water. He turns and runs down the trail toward the beach. He stumbles on the rough terrain but continues into the forest, legs churning as if through cement, heart pounding, lungs starved for oxygen, eyes swimming. The trees thin as the land rises and ahead he can see a figure silhouetted against the moonlit water. His lungs burn. He pushes harder.

■ ■ ■

From the cliff top, Timmons watches Liz land in the water with a huge splash, and eventually surface, alive and kicking, swimming down the shoreline.

"Fucking bitch!"

Timmons hesitates; it's a long way down. He braces himself, then jumps, arms windmilling. Timmons lands in the water slightly off-kilter, behind Liz. Half-stunned, he surfaces, overhauls her, just grabbing her foot. She takes a breath and dives down and they struggle under the water. Liz knees him in the balls and swims to the surface, sucks in a lungful of air. Timmons grabs her instantly, drags her under. Liz breaks free again and strokes for shore, kicking out with her foot and feeling it strike Timmons' nose with a satisfying crunch. She makes it to the shallows of the rocky beach. Timmons galumphs up onto her in the shallows, grabs her hair from behind and pulls her head back, punches her in the kidneys and knocks Liz down. She screams in pain and anger.

Liz and Timmons fight in the shallow, rock-strewn water—a brutal struggle, no holds barred, teeth, nails, anything. His hands all over her. She fights ferociously, gouging at his face, but he is too strong for her. She falls again into the shallow water, on her back. Timmons raises a barnacle-encrusted rock to crush Liz's skull.

A shot rings out. Timmons freezes, unharmed. The rock still poised above Liz, Timmons turns toward shore and the sound of the shot—at Jack Harris, standing on the beach. Jack's first shot has missed, his hand trembling. Jack holds the gun with two hands, steadying it at Timmons chest.

"Who the *fuck* are you?" screams Timmons.

"I'm the last sonofabitch you're ever going to see on this earth, pardner."

"You can't just shoot me. This is Canada."

Jack smiles. "I'm an American, asshole."

Focusing on the front sight, letting the target blur slightly, Jack drills him center-mass with a hundred and fifty-eight grains of .357 Magnum copper-jacketed hollow-point bullet. Timmons is instantly blown over, lying face-up in the shallow water beside Liz, lifeless eyes staring into the darkness.

Liz staggers up, coughing, wiping the blood out of her eyes, sees Jack on the beach, silhouetted against the lightening sky, holding his stubby AirLite .357 Magnum ankle gun.

Jack wades into the shallows and helps Liz up. "Are you okay?"

Liz checks Timmons' pulse. "Better than Timmons. Fucking hell."

"I figured you were worth saving." Jack gives her his jacket.

"Thanks, Jack. I owe you one." She looks at his pistol. "Thought you said you only had a shotgun."

Jack smiles wryly. "I never said that. You didn't ask me about a pistol."

"Where do you think Knifeblade is?"

"I don't know, but it can't be good."

The sound of an outboard motor cuts into their conversation. Liz looks up and sees a small aluminum boat approaching in the gray dawn, driven by Fouché.

Liz looks at Fouché. "Perfect timing. The Mountie arrives to save the day."

The boat lands and Fouché jumps out, wades ashore.

"Liz, my God! Are you all right?"

"Yes, but barely."

Fouché sees the body lying in the shallows. "Oh, Jesus. I assume that's Timmons."

"Yes," says Liz. "He tried to kill me. How'd you get here so fast? We haven't even called it in."

"I knew something was up when you didn't return my call. Had to commandeer a boat. Got here as soon as I could." Fouché examines Timmons' body. "Damn, guess we won't get anything out of him."

"Not without a séance," says Jack.

"Would have been nice to know where the bodies are."

Jack looks across the cove at Timmons' boathouse. Below the boathouse is the beach where Bob and Daisy found Amanda's foot. Then he looks out at the bay.

"I think I know."

23

RCMP diver Dick MacLean jumps into the frigid water from an RIB Zodiac. He adjusts his regulator, clears his mask, exhales and lets the air out of his buoyancy compensator, sinking down into the dark, green water, following the clean yellow line of the RCMP buoy marker. He shines his light around, the yellow beam cutting through the turbidity and plankton. MacLean can hear the sucking of his regulator, the sound of the bubbles rushing past, clearing his ears, the crinkly compression of the dry suit around his body as he sinks.

The gray, muddy bottom resolves into view beneath him and suddenly something pale looms up below, waving softly with the current like yellow eel grass. Only it isn't eel grass at all. It's human hair, blond human hair, attached to a blanched, nude female body floating languidly in the current, chained to something, her arms rising above her. And beside her more corpses appear out of the gloom, all blond, all nude—a forest of nude bodies in different states of decay. Each one more ghastly than the other. Their hands swaying above them in the current like branches of a tree. All tethered to anchors with heavy chains. And all missing a foot. Crabs, shrimp, small green fishes and copepods swarm around the flesh, feeding. One girl more recent than the rest, blond hair floating above her lovely, ghostly frame. Beside her is a male body as well—still clothed and with both feet intact—a heavy beard and dark, matted hair. The whole thing a gruesome underwater sculpture as if carefully placed to move with the tides, a macabre underwater ballet choreographed by a madman. MacLean, an experienced police diver, begins to hyperventilate, sucking hard on the regulator, which does not seem to be delivering air as it should. He feels the bile rush into his throat, quickly swims to the surface, exhaling bubbles all the way.

24

Months later, Richards is looking through the old Timmons files in Conference Room B. On a dolly, there are several case-file boxes, neatly stacked to go to storage. Fouché pops his head into the conference room.

"Want to go get a drink?"

"No, I have a few things I want to finish up," says Richards.

"What's to finish?"

"I don't know. Something's bugging me."

"Why? Coroner's Inquest returned a verdict of justifiable homicide. As far as Jack Harris is concerned, he fired to protect an officer in the line of duty. Our IA guys came to the same conclusion, and he gets a Section 10 dismissal on the unregistered firearms charge." says Fouché. "That's good enough for me. It was a clean shoot."

"*Sort* of clean. Kind of fits his old MO, don't you think? Shoot first, ask questions later?"

"So what? Harris acted in self-defense, or at least in defense of Liz. A serial killer gets taken off the board, Liz and RCMP get away clean. Timmons was a very bad actor we're all better off without, and no messy trial where things can drag on for years, and not always work out. What's not to like?"

"That's not all that's bothering me," says Richards.

"Then what else?"

"I've been looking over Zach's forensics report . . ." Richards shuffles through a file folder. "There is absolutely no forensic evidence in that boathouse—no trace of blood or hair or DNA—other than Timmons and Liz. That's just not possible. I don't care how careful you are, how much cleanup you do, you cut up fourteen people, there has to be something, some blood or DNA somewhere. Plus, the timeline doesn't play."

"What timeline?"

Richards scrolls through his notebook. "According to Liz, she hears Bob Carter's dog going bonkers around 2:00 AM. She gets to the island around 2:10. Harris follows shortly thereafter, takes him a little longer, in his kayak. Timmons ambushes Liz a few minutes later, ties her up and then leaves her to get his collection of sex-torture tools or whatever. She has time to get out of her restraints and hide by the time he comes back. She figures less than ten minutes. Then she runs, he chases her off the cliff, they struggle and Timmons gets shot by Harris. So far so good. Right?"

Fouché shrugs. "That's what is says in the report."

"Okay. If Daisy started barking when something happened to Bob Carter—Knifeblade—when did *Timmons* have time to kill Bob—*and then* dump his body in the bay? The guy was chained to an anchor beside all the other bodies, several hundred yards out, in the middle of the bay, right? You'd have to take a small boat out to do that. So when did Timmons have time to do it? And let's just say he does have time? How come Harris doesn't see Timmons dumping the bodies on his way over to the island?"

"Okay. It was dark. Maybe Timmons did it the day *before* and Knifeblade's dog was barking just because dogs bark." Fouché frowns. "You don't buy Jack Harris's story? Or Liz's, for that matter?"

"Maybe. I don't know. Something kind of hinky about the whole thing. My Spidey sense is telling me. We never interviewed all of Amanda's teammates. According to my notes, one of them may have got a look at the boyfriend."

"Well, Spiderman, there *is* something hinky about Jack Harris. I agree with you there."

"Maybe so. But it still doesn't answer why there is no DNA from Bob or anybody else in that boathouse. I want to go out there and check it again."

"Do you want me to come with you?"

"No, I've got it. But thanks. I'll head over first thing tomorrow."

25

Jack peruses the crowd. A teen runaway, a down-on-his-luck guy with a bad tie, a prostitute trying to get out of the life. His thoughts drift. *How did each of them get to where they are today? The runaway thumbing her way to the city from an isolated farm. Escaping a drunk father who can't keep his hands to himself. The hooker who lost her kids because she smokes crack. Looks fifty but is only thirty. What kind of job is she going to get based on her résumé? The man with the tie and hand-me-down suit, a hopeless case if there ever was one, still coming off his last drunk.* Jack imagines him trying to put his best foot forward at a job interview, his clothes betraying his lot. *The interviewer would never give this guy a shot. Hard holes to climb out of.*

"Jack . . . Jack . . ."

Jack snaps back to the present. He feels the coin in his hand, smooth and cool and then he stands and walks to the rostrum. The crowd stares at him. He has to steady himself, gather his thoughts.

"I am here because, ah, I have thirty days under my belt and my sponsor says the next step is to tell my story."

He looks across the room to Rosie, who smiles and nods in encouragement.

"I'm generally not one to follow rules but if any of you know Rosie, you would shape up quick too."

Chuckles from the room.

Jack clears his throat. "Unfortunately, for the moment, this is all I have to say—My name is Jack and, ah, I'm an alcoholic."

The room responds, "Hi, Jack."

Rosie takes a drag on her cigarette.

26

Jack takes the ferry home that evening. The air is cool and damp, darkness coming early as the sun sinks into the hulking mountains of Vancouver Island to the west, already dusted with the first snows of fall. He takes out his cell phone, steps into the shelter of the big, empty cabin, and dials her number.

Liz answers. "MacDonald."

"Liz, it's Jack."

"Oh, hi . . . Jack! How's it going?"

"Just got my thirty-day chip. I feel like celebrating. Join me for drinks?"

"*Seriously?*"

"Just kidding. I'm good. On the ferry home actually, clean and sober. Why I called you, I finished *Skookum*."

"Skookum?"

"My boat. I'm taking her up the coast for a week or so, kind of a shakedown cruise. I remember you mentioned you might like to visit Desolation Sound . . . It's gorgeous up there this time of year . . . And, um, we've got a good weather window coming up, so . . ." He trails off lamely.

"Jack, that's really sweet . . ."

"But . . ."

"I don't know, Jack."

"I'll be the perfect gentleman. I swear."

"That's what I'm afraid of. No, seriously . . . Not sure I can get the time off. We still have a lot of missing persons to find . . ."

"Maybe we can find some of them up in Desolation Sound."

"Wow, you really know the way to a girl's heart. Offer to take her sailing on a romantic wooden sailboat, promise not touch her, and maybe we can look for some missing persons."

"That's me. A true romantic at heart."

"Should I bring a cadaver dog?"

"Good thinking. But Daisy will do. Meet me on the island, day after tomorrow. Or I can sail over to Vancouver, if you like."

She sighs. Takes a deep breath. "Okay, you win, assuming I can swing it with Ward. They owe me some time, I guess. I'll come to you. Day after tomorrow."

"Fantastic, Liz."

"What should I bring? Bottle of wine?"

"Um, not such a good—"

"Kidding . . ."

"Right. Just bring warm clothes; it gets chilly up there this time of year. I'll get the groceries."

He says goodbye and hangs up. Smiles. It's the first time in a while. The sun drops out from behind the clouds over the island, briefly lights up the western sky with a blaze of fire, and then sinks beneath the mountains, leaving the land beneath, and the islands ahead, in darkness.

■ ■ ■

In the morning, Richards is at Timmons' boathouse, walking past tatters of old crime scene tape. He enters the darkened boathouse. From a shelf, he grabs a rusty hammer and starts prying up floorboards, shining his flashlight around. His phone rings.

"This is Richards."

"It's Zach. Gone over everything twice as you requested . . ."

"And?"

"Still nothing new. Just DNA matching Timmons and Liz. Sorry."

"That can't be right. There must be some trace evidence."

"Sorry. Nothing."

"Okay. Thanks. Let me know if anything comes up."

"Will do."

Richards hangs up his cell. He walks onto the dock, looks back at Timmons' boathouse, desolate, its crime scene tape vibrating in the wind, like an empty stage after the actors have left and the lights are turned off. He turns and looks across the bay, past the RCMP buoy where the bodies were found, toward Jack's cabin—the light is on in the gathering dusk. Richards then looks to the other side of the cove—directly across from Timmons' boathouse. A few hundred yards down the beach from where he's standing is another summer home, its windows boarded up. And near it, built out over the water on a rickety pier, another boathouse. Very much like Timmons'.

Richards hesitates, clambers down the dock onto the beach and trudges through the wet gravel, low-tide wrack and old kelp toward the other boathouse, somewhat more dilapidated than Timmons'. A distant foghorn sounds. He bangs on the locked door.

"RCMP! . . . Police!"

There is no response. Richards shines his light through the cracks of the boarded-up window, but can see nothing. He looks around and shoulders open the door, breaking the flimsy lock, enters, gun and flashlight drawn. A deserted maze of beams, ropes and chains, boating gear, faint light shining in through cracked windows, reflecting up from the water. Otherwise empty. Still. Richards rounds a corner into an alcove, stops dead, recoils at what he sees.

"Christ!"

Before him is a stainless steel fish-cleaning table, with four leather restraints bolted to the sides. Surgical instruments are laid out neatly on a side table. Visqueen plastic is rolled out underneath the table as a tidy drop cloth. A blue tarp is neatly folded on a shelf. And in a corner, a video camera set up on a tripod sees it all. The little red light on the camera lens blinks, a single red snake eye in the gloom.

"Oh, fuck . . ."

Richards turns away in horror, and stops dead, sees the figure in the doorway, instinctively draws his gun but there's a moment's hesitation, he holds fire—his last mistake—just as the dart hits him in the neck. Richards' gun fires almost simultaneously but the shot goes wide. Richards staggers, looks at his gun incredulously, touching the dart in his neck tentatively, the world irises in and Richards crashes to the floor.

27

Liz has the TV on to the CBC in her bedroom as she is packing up her bag. Sweaters, fleece, jeans, socks, underwear, boat shoes, Gore-Tex parka, gloves, wool beanie and a set of long johns, just in case. Finds her point-and-shoot camera and charger. She jumps into the shower just as a news report comes on.

The reporter dramatically states, "Today another severed foot was found in the Gulf Islands. DNA testing is underway to see if it matches any of the previous victims linked to the Severed Foot Killer, William Timmons. The RCMP declined to comment further. In other news . . ."

But Liz cannot hear with the water running. The story ends just as Liz walks back into the bedroom, rubbing her hair with a towel. Liz grabs the remote and turns the TV off. She takes one last look at the clothing in her duffle and then zips it up.

■ ■ ■

On the ferry, Liz enjoys the view of the Gulf Islands. The air is fresh but not too cold, sky still clear and dry. About fifteen knots of northwesterly breeze. Perfect fall weather. Her phone rings.

"MacDonald."

"Liz, it's Fouché. Listen, have you heard from Richards?"

"No, why?"

"He didn't turn up for work and he isn't answering his cell."

"That doesn't sound like Frank. I haven't heard from him but I'm actually on vacation. On the ferry now."

"Oh. I won't bother you then. Where are you going?"

"Don't know yet."

"Okay . . ."

"Doug, let me know if he doesn't turn up. I should have cell service."

"Have a good time, Liz."

"Thanks, Doug. I will."

■ ■ ■

On Jack's island, the air is crisp and smells of wood-smoke and pulp from a nearby mill and the hardwood leaves have turned brilliant oranges, reds and yellows. Jack's little wooden sailboat *Skookum* is fully restored to all its former, if modest, glory. All thirty-two feet newly painted, varnished, overhauled and lovingly readied for sea, rocking gently at her dock, tugging at her mooring lines. Liz and Jack walk down the dock with Daisy.

"Nice boat, Skipper!"

"A boat is a hole in the water into which money is poured."

Liz looks in a bag of groceries on deck. "No Macallan?"

"Damn. Must have forgotten it."

"So, Desolation Sound still on the cruise itinerary?"

"Yep. If you're up for it. It's cold up there this time of year, but . . ."

"I think we can find a way to stay warm. I can give you handcuff lessons."

Jack smiles. "It'll be just the two of us."

They load up, cast off and sail away from Jack's island, heading north, past the small marker buoy in the middle of the bay.

■ ■ ■

The first day goes quickly, in fine weather, chugging along through the calm water on the little inboard diesel, out of the maze of the Gulf Islands. They clear Pylades, Ruxton and Decourcy Islands, working through Gabriola Pass, between Valdes Island and Gabriola on a swift outgoing tide, leaving Thrasher Rock to port. The wind comes up as they motor out into the Strait of Georgia—or the Salish Sea, as it's now called—a pleasant northwesterly, about twelve to fifteen knots, just enough to raise whitecaps.

Jack hands her a foul-weather jacket, gives her the tiller, and goes forward to raise the main.

"Are we expecting a storm?

"Nope. But you'll get cold from the wind. Take the tiller. Just keep her steady into the eye of the wind. Slack off the mainsheet first, please."

"Aye, Cap'n, yar! Haven't got a clue what you are talking about, Cap'n!"

"The red rope, there on that winch."

"Who are you calling a wench? This one?"

"Yep, just slack it off a bit till I get the sail up. Hold her into the wind!"

Liz does her best and the sail rises flapping into the breeze.

"Okay, belay the mainsheet—pull in the red line—and cleat her off. Just wrap it round that cleat, a round turn'll do. Now fall off."

"Won't it be cold?"

"It means turn a bit off the wind, to starboard, smart-ass—to your right. The other right."

Liz gets the feel for the ass-backwards way the tiller works, and the boat pays off the breeze, heels over as Jack cranks the mainsheet in hard and kills the engine. The lovely quiet settles in. He un-cleats the jib furling line and pulls in the leeward jib sheet, unrolling the roller-furling jib, and the boat heels further, eliciting a squeal of alarm and then delight from Liz as the boat comes alive for the first time in the resounding silence absent the clamor of the motor. The boat heels still further as Jack swiftly trims the jib, but lifting now, surging forward, accelerating and bending to her true purpose in the world, like a thoroughbred given her head to run.

Liz smiles. "This is fantastic! Is it supposed to lean over this much?"

"Yep. That's only about fifteen degrees of heel." Jack glances up at the telltales, makes an adjustment on the main. "You're doing fine, just keep her so, steer about twenty degrees magnetic."

"Magnetic?"

"By the compass, or just aim for that mountain on the island over there. That'll work. Now we're sailing, by God!"

"It's wonderful . . . You actually know how to run this thing, right?"

"Not my first rodeo, sugar."

"Yar!"

Once Liz realizes they're not going to capsize, she begins to relax and enjoy herself. They tack up the Strait of Georgia into open water, the breeze freshening, the boat dipping to the small closely spaced whitecaps, beginning to throw spray to leeward, lee rail just dipping under, and around noon Jack takes a reef in the main and rolls up the jib a turn or two to balance her in. *Skookum*, heeling less now, finds her rhythm and works her way up the Strait, past ragged Lasquiti Island, the long bulk of Texada looming above.

They make Comox at sunset on the first day. In the last of the breeze, Jack takes her over the tricky and very shallow, rock studded-bar under just the main, following the buoys carefully, turns to port once clear of the bar, and brings her to anchor under sail behind the lee of Denman Island, in about five fathoms of water, just at sunset.

"We're not going into Comox?" says Liz. "No shore excursion for the cruise ship passengers?"

"Nah. Let's anchor out here—we've got the whole anchorage to ourselves. I'm kind of done with cities for a while."

"Right, Skipper. The mean streets of Comox, eh?"

They take Daisy ashore in the dinghy for a pee and a walk on the oyster-crunching shingle in their rubber boots. Birds wheel and cry above them on the desolate spit. After, Jack makes them a simple dinner of barbequed salmon and a salad and warmed sourdough bread, using a nifty little stainless barbeque bolted to the stern rail. Washing it down with bottled water and coffee. It's all incredibly good and for some reason Liz has a huge appetite. The dusk falls slowly, and then full dark descends; thousands of stars appear overhead, so many it makes Liz dizzy just to look at them. In the cockpit, Liz snuggles into the crook of Jack's arm, still on deck despite the chill breeze dropping off the glaciers in the mountains above Comox. They are the only boat in the anchorage. True to his word, he makes no move toward her, besides this warm and pleasant and companionable snuggling. It is enough. For both of them.

Eventually, she turns in, curling up in a sleeping bag alone in the settee berth amidships. He takes the V-berth forward among the spare sails and anchor lines and other gear stored there. Liz feels the creak of the wooden boat working gently at her mooring, listening to the little wavelets hollow-slap against the hull, the flatter slap of the halyards on the mast in the gentle land breeze, rocked gently in the cradle of the boat. She falls asleep in about twenty seconds.

28

Two days later, Jack sails *Skookum* into the wilderness of Desolation Sound, overlapping layers of misty islands and big, dark peaks looming in the distance above long, narrow fjords. The boat leans into the wind on a broad reach, her sails taut as she cuts through the water at a nice clip. Ominous dark clouds pile up in the northwestern sky. After they had cleared Comox Bar, the wind had come round out of the southeast and carried them at a brisk six knots across the Strait, in about five hours, past the northern tip of Texada, leaving Harwood Island to starboard, Savary to port. They entered the little marina at Lund for supplies and hot showers. The weather was colder and beginning to cloud up with big cirrus high in the stratosphere, yet remained dry. Liz wore her gloves and a wool beanie.

Jack remained friendly, kidding and joshing her, even flirting with her, but not overly sexual. Slightly awkward, in fact. It was beginning to drive Liz crazy.

In tiny Lund, the last town on the end of Canada Highway 1, they stocked up on supplies, had their showers and enjoyed incredibly good scones and cappuccinos at Nancy's Bakery, but Jack would not spend the night in Lund, hemmed in with all the other boats. They fueled up at the gas dock and worked out of the little harbor, sailed about two miles north and tucked into a gunkhole in the shelter of the Copeland Islands for the night.

Now, they sail across the Sound into Stag Bay, on Hernando Island, anchoring in about ten fathoms with a stern line ashore, nicely sheltered from the southeast breeze.

"We'll be okay here if a storm comes? Looks like rain, Skipper."

"We'll be fine as long as this southeaster holds. If the wind shifts, we'll have to clear out and go around to Baker's Front or get into Cortes Bay, right over there. But I think it will hold. Rain tomorrow though."

Later that evening, Jack and Liz enjoy the view of the glacier-clad mountains rising up out of the layers of islands in the sound to the northeast. It's a gray, cold evening, and Liz is wearing her long johns.

A whooshing *pfipht!* sound—Jack looks up at the familiar spouts of killer whales and the long black dorsal fins cutting through the darkening water.

"Look!" says Jack. "Orcas. Two males, a couple of juveniles and three females."

"Oh my God! That's incredible!"

The orcas enter the bay, darkly sinister, moving purposefully toward them, passing *Skookum* by a few yards and cavort for a while in the shallows, spouting, blowing and rubbing themselves on the gravel of the beach, rolling against the scratchy barnacled rocks in just a few feet of water. Liz grabs her camera and snaps photos.

"I think I know these guys . . ." says Jack. "I saw the same pod a few months back, kayaking. Same markings on that big male."

"They're kind of scary, aren't they? I mean I know they don't attack people, but, my God . . . Look at the size of that fin!"

"We're not in Kansas anymore, Toto. They look a little different a few feet away, from the deck of a small boat, don't they? They're carnivores. This is the wild. We're no longer at the top of the food chain."

After a time, as if by some prearranged signal, the orcas turn and head off toward a small islet at the other end of the bay, hunting sea lions perhaps, their spouts and knifing fins cutting the green and placid surface of the water, leaving a rippling wake.

Jack looks at Liz. "You're awfully quiet."

"Something's bothering me."

"The orcas?"

"No. Not that. That was amazing."

"What then? Ship's entertainment not up to snuff? Food not to your standards, m'lady? I would write a sternly worded letter to the captain at once."

"No. This cruise is grand. This is shop talk."

"Shop talk?"

"Yes. Why did Timmons kill Bob? It's completely out of his profile."

Jack sighs, shrugs. "Bob probably walked in on something—or saw something he shouldn't have—and Timmons had to kill him."

"Okay, *when* did he do it? How did Timmons have time to kill Bob *and* dump the body in the bay?"

"Well . . . We don't know what Daisy was barking at initially—or for that matter when Bob was actually killed. The two events may not be related. Bob could have been killed the day before. Make sense?"

Liz looks at him. "I guess so. But it still bugs me. Why didn't he cut off Bob's foot?"

"I don't know . . . Maybe because Bob's not a blond female runner. Sometimes everything doesn't wrap up with a nice neat bow."

Daisy whines.

"I need to take her on shore, for a walk. Maybe I'll try to catch us some dinner."

"Okay. I think I'll curl up with a cup of tea and a book."

"Murder mystery?"

"No, thanks. I prefer bodice-rippers."

Jack smiles. "Me too."

"Jack, can I ask you something personal?"

"Shoot."

"How much longer is this perfect gentleman act going to last?"

Jack smiles, looks away, then back to her. "I thought you'd never ask. Not much longer, I'm beginning to run out of excuses."

She smiles. "Good. It's starting to drive me nuts. I may have to write a sternly worded letter to the captain."

He kisses her right then. Softly, almost chastely on the lips. Looks her in the eyes. Daisy barks. She kisses him back hard and for real, the warm wet softness of her lips, the heat of her mouth, the insistent press of her body and clinging arms, the firmness of her small breasts and crinkling nipples pressing into him, her touch, and the heady astonishing scent of her—and the world begins to spin. Daisy barks again.

Jack comes up for air, catches his breath. "I guess she won't wait."

"Okay, whew. That was close. Thanks, Daisy. You bitch."

"She's just jealous. Another blonde, after all. I'd better take her ashore. Be right back."

"Okay, but if you don't come back in five minutes exactly, I'm going to sail this boat into Lund without you and roger the first lumberjack I can find."

"Yes, ma'am. Back in five minutes exactly."

Jack coaxes Daisy into the dinghy tied alongside. Liz waves at them as they row away.

■ ■ ■

Below deck, Liz fills a pot with some water and puts it on the stove. Her hands are a little shaky. She looks in one of the cabinets for a tea bag. The box is empty, so she looks in another drawer under the chart table. She rummages through a bottom drawer—it's stuck, so she yanks on it and the drawer pops open revealing a large knife in a sheath. *Odd . . .* She picks it up, taking it out of its sheath—stares at the blade with horror. It is Knifeblade Bob's custom-made, one-of-a-kind, twisted strands of 440C stainless steel bridge cable knife, cold to the touch, like ice. A jolt goes through her arm, as if the knife were electrified. She drops it back into the drawer, sits staring at it dumbly for a few moments, trying to comprehend, knowing perfectly well what it means but unwilling to believe it. Through the porthole she sees Jack land the dinghy on the little shell beach, Daisy hopping out into the shallows, running up into the grass.

Liz takes out her cell phone. No service. She turns to the boat's VHF radio and sees a label: *Marine Operator— Channel 22.* She turns the radio on and turns to Channel 22.

"Marine operator. Marine operator. This is Corporal MacDonald, RCMP."

The operator crackles on the other end. "Marine operator."

"Please patch me in to RCMP in Vancouver. I need to speak to Corporal Doug Fouché. This is a police emergency."

"Stand-by, please."

After a short pause, the RCMP operator picks up and transfers the call.

"Corporal Fouché."

"Fouché, it's Liz. Thank God you're there. Listen to me." She's a little out of breath. "I'm with Jack Harris on his boat, up in Desolation Sound. I found something!"

"What? Say again? You cut out there."

"Can you hear me now? I found—"

"Yes, I can hear you. Go ahead, Liz."

"I found Knifeblade Bob's knife on Jack Harris' boat!"

"What? Whose knife?'

"Knifeblade Bob—the caretaker on Francisco Island. It's his knife. It's one-of-a-kind."

"Jesus. Are you sure?"

"Dead sure. Bob wore it on his belt. He showed it to me. He told me he hand-made it out of a piece of steel bridge cable." Liz glances through the porthole, sees Jack putting Daisy into the dinghy, pushing off, rowing toward the boat.

"What are you saying, Liz?"

"I don't know. It means . . . I don't know what it means. How did it get here?"

"There's got to be a logical explanation."

"The knife wasn't on Bob's body. The only person who could have that knife is the killer . . ."

"But this makes no sense. What about Timmons? We *know* he tried to kill you and he killed Bob too, didn't he?"

"What if Timmons didn't kill Bob?" says Liz. "Maybe Timmons was just a rapist who happened to be on Francisco Island."

"Two killers on one island in the same night? Or one killer and a rapist, whatever. Seems like a stretch."

"I know. But I'm alone on a boat with Jack and a stainless steel knife in the middle of nowhere."

"Liz, listen. Something's happened you should know about. Another foot washed ashore near Jack's island. We think it's Richards'."

"Why do you think that?"

"The shoe matches the cheap old sneakers he would wear to the gym. We think he wore them to the crime scene at the boathouse because he didn't want to muck up his street shoes on the beach. He went out there to check on something, five days ago, and hasn't turned up since. Officially listed as missing. It's too coincidental. Zach is running DNA as we speak."

"Oh, fuck. Listen, I have to sign off. Jack's ashore right now with the dog. He'll be back in about a minute."

"Where are you?"

Liz looks at a chart. "Ah . . . We are in a place called Stag Bay, on Hernando Island, about five miles northwest of Lund. Only boat for miles . . ."

"Can you get off the boat? Get ashore somehow without him?"

"I doubt it. Not without raising his suspicions. It's too cold to swim for it."

"You don't happen to have your firearm with you do you?"

"Of course not. I'm off-duty. You know the rules. I wasn't expecting a gunfight."

"Right. Sorry, didn't mean to alarm you. Sit tight. I'll get there as quickly as I can. I'll get a chopper or a plane. Stay cool, Liz. I'm sure there's another explanation but don't do anything to provoke him. Just be cool."

Liz ends the call with the marine operator, puts the mike back on its hook and suddenly the tea kettle whistles, making Liz jump. Jack is standing in the companionway.

She slowly shuts the drawer the knife is lying in with her foot, hoping that she's hiding it with her body. Not sure how much he heard.

Jack regards the radio, still on and blaring static. "What's up?"

Liz fiddles with it. "Just trying to check the weather report."

Jack climbs down the companion ladder, turns the kettle down and then points to a button on the radio marked *WX*.

"Just press this button."

He looks at her strangely. The weather report comes on. *"Rain and high winds predicted for the waters of Desolation Sound. Small craft warnings are in effect for the Salish Sea . . ."*

Jack pours himself a cup of tea, glances at the chart. "I want to up-anchor. Let's move up the Sound. It'll be much quieter there."

"Jack, we're the only boat in the cove."

Jack looks at the chart. "Let's go to Waterfall Cove. Better holding ground, and more protected. Storm's coming. We should find a better anchorage."

"Really? That's another twenty miles away, and if there's going to be a storm . . ."

Jack smiles. "You're Canadian. A little rain won't bother you. Besides, it's got a great waterfall. And there's no one around for miles."

Distant thunder rumbles. "There you go. Right on cue. Didn't you want some tea?" says Jack.

29

Skookum sails up the darkening fjord toward Waterfall Cove, into the Sound proper, under a moody gray sky. The wind picks up, blowing out of the southeast, heeling the little sloop over on a broad reach till the lee rail touches the water—spray coming aboard.

Jack winches in the jib sheet, checking the chart for hidden rocks and shoals, navigating carefully up the narrowing fjord. Liz regards him warily. She's cold but doesn't go below deck. The dark wall of a squall approaches from the head of the fjord, spiked with lightning. Rain begins to patter on the deck.

■ ■ ■

The RCMP Cessna 185 floatplane takes a maddening hour and a half to make it up the coast toward Desolation Sound, buffeting and jinking in the rising wind, scudding low under the dark rain clouds. Fouché is riding in the front seat with the pilot. Rain begins to spatter and streak back off the windshield in the slipstream. Map in hand, Fouché has the pilot fly over Hernando Island, making a low pass. Stag Bay is empty. No boat in sight.

"Shit. They have to be somewhere . . . Let's check Cortes Bay, then head northeast. Up into the Sound."

"Okay . . . But I don't like the looks of that weather," says the pilot into his headset. "Have to head back pretty soon."

The plane makes a pass over the open water, flying over Cortes Bay. A few fishing boats and some larger yachts are anchored in the middle of the bay, but no sign of Jack's sailboat. The pilot banks into a tight 360, climbs for a bit of altitude, heads further up the Sound. Big dark clouds of a squall advance down the inlet, blocking the fjord a few miles ahead. The pilot spots a small sailing boat, a little white arrow of wood and sail, cutting a wake through the green chop below them. He flies overhead, turns back, descends giddily and makes a low pass. The plane shudders as they roar over the boat.

"That's them!"

■ ■ ■

Liz and Jack notice the RCMP floatplane pass overhead, turn and then drop in for a flyby, as if on a strafing run.

"That's weird. I wonder what's going on."

Liz says, "Maybe there was a boating accident. They must be looking for someone."

"Maybe. Haven't heard anything on the radio."

Rain spatters them on deck, big drops now whipped by the rising wind into their faces.

"Let's reef the main in case this wind picks up. We may be in for a bit of a squall. Why don't you head below and secure anything that's loose."

"Maybe we should turn around, head back to Hernando."

"Nah. We're fine. It's only a few more miles to Waterfall Cove."

"Okay, Jack."

■ ■ ■

Fouché braces himself against the juddering turbulence, craning his neck to look down on the small boat as it flashes past through the scud. The little plane is buffeted around by the wind.

"Can you land nearby? It's an emergency."

The pilot dismisses the suggestion. "Too rough now in this wind. Look at the waves." He points at the oncoming storm. "And no way we can fly through that squall. And if we did set down someplace, we'll never get off again until this storm passes. I'll set you down in Lund and you can rent a boat from there. Assuming you can get someone to rent you one in this weather."

The pilot turns the plane around.

"Where's the nearest RCMP unit?" asks Fouché.

"Powell River. Want me to call the Coast Guard?"

"No. I'll handle it."

■ ■ ■

The floatplane lands in the sheltered water in front of Lund, taxis up to the red-painted government dock. Fouché steps out, waves off the pilot and heads over to a boat rental dock. The pilot turns the plane away from the dock with a blast of the prop that washes over Fouché and takes away his hat.

The boat rental guy is closing up shop. Fouché flashes his badge, and the man unlocks the door.

"I need a boat, please. Police emergency."

Within minutes, Fouché is at the helm of a small rented fishing boat, pounding up through the chop, past the shelter of the Copeland Islands, into the Sound.

30

Seen from afar, Jack's anchored boat is a dot of light, a single glow of warmth in a darkening wilderness with the big waterfall thundering across the smooth, sheltered water of the inlet. Jack admires the beautiful waterfall from the cockpit.

"Look at this. Isn't it amazing? Worth coming up here for, eh? And this is an all-weather anchorage. Normally there'd be tons of boats in here but now we've got it all to ourselves. Then maybe we can finish our unfinished business."

He smiles, puts his arm around Liz. She tries not to recoil. Rain and fog are rolling in. Jack reacts to her sudden mood change.

"What's wrong, Liz?"

"I think I've caught a chill. I'm going below."

Liz goes below and puts the kettle on.

■ ■ ■

Fouché, on his rented fishing boat, battered, half seasick, freezing cold and soaked through with rain and spray from his fifteen-mile bash up the Sound in a borrowed foul-weather jacket, approaches Waterfall Cove. He nearly runs aground on a rock in the narrow entrance, veers off the looming shoal, throttles back on the outboard. There is a single anchored sailboat deep inside the placid black water of the cove, sheltered from all winds, its anchor light gleaming in the dusk, portholes lit from within.

He blows into his freezing hands, wipes his face with a boat towel.

"How romantic . . ."

He putters up, calls out, "Ahoy, *Skookum*! RCMP! Prepare to be boarded!"

Jack sticks his head up the hatch. Looks at Fouché, surprised. "Sure. Come on aboard."

He turns to Liz. "Isn't that your partner? What's this about?"

Liz sticks her head out of the hatch. Looks at Fouché, back at Jack. "No idea."

Fouché bumps rudely up alongside, throws Jack a bowline, and climbs aboard. Daisy barks.

"Quiet, Daisy," says Jack. "Corporal Fouché. This is a pleasant surprise."

Fouché looks closely at Liz. "Liz, are you okay?"

"I'm fine."

Jack glances from one to the other. "Why wouldn't she be? What's going on?"

"There's been a new development in the foot case."

"This couldn't wait until we got back?"

"I'm afraid not."

"You came all the way from Lund in that thing? In this weather?"

"Yes. Nearly swamped. It was touch and go a couple of times. But really, I had no choice."

"How did you know where we were?"

"Liz called me."

"Why?"

"Just to check in."

Jack looks at Liz, back at Fouché. "Okay, come below. I'll put coffee on."

They go below, leaving Daisy on deck. Jack puts the kettle on, makes them coffee. Liz sits at the chart table. Daisy barks from the deck above.

Jack yells, "Daisy, *quiet*!" He looks at Fouché. "So let me guess, another foot turned up?"

Fouché sits at the little dinette, his back to the bulkhead, facing both of them. "Good guess. Just before you left, in fact. I'm surprised you didn't hear of it."

"One of Timmons' earlier victims?"

"I don't think so. It's fresh."

"Where did it wash up?"

"Just off your island, as it turns out. And Richards is missing, I'm sorry to say."

"Really? Richards? Then we've got a copycat."

"I doubt it. You were pretty clever, Jack. Calling in that first foot. You even said we should put you on the suspect list." Fouché pauses, absently scratching his lower leg.

Jack looks around. Liz stands in the companionway. Fouché is still seated calmly at the end of the table.

"Excuse me?" says Jack. "What the *hell* are you talking about?"

"It's pretty slick. You incorporate yourself into the investigation. You move around, operating from different boathouses in the islands. Choose your victims carefully. Easy, until Bob caught you . . . You get rid of Bob, then, while 'saving' Liz, you shoot Timmons, the only suspect. I assume that gun was your old throw-down. But you made one mistake."

Fouché leans over toward the chart table beside Liz, without taking his eyes off of Jack, opens the bottom drawer and pulls out Bob's knife and slams it onto the table.

"You took Bob's one-of-a-kind knife."

Jack takes a step back. He studies Fouché intently. Glances at Liz. A long, hard glance.

"Don't you mean," says Jack, "this is where *you* made a mistake?"

"Excuse me?"

"I have no idea how that knife got there. I didn't put it there. Liz, did you?"

"No."

Jack glances from one to the other. Fouché smiles.

"Nice try, Jack," says Fouché.

"Fouché. One question: How did you know that knife was in *that* drawer? Did you tell him, Liz?"

Liz is stunned. "No. I . . . No, definitely not."

Fouché looks at Liz. Then at Jack, smiling sheepishly. Jack lunges suddenly for Fouché, who pulls a large, futuristic-looking pistol from within his jacket and points it at Jack. Jack freezes.

"Where'd you get the dart gun, Doug?"

"What, this old thing? The Internet."

Liz is in shock. "Oh my God. Jack, I'm so sorry."

Fouché smiles and shoots Jack with a dart in the chest, the gun making a sudden *pfist* sound. Jack struggles to get to Fouché before the dart kicks in, gets a hand on his shoulder but collapses in a heap on the cabin sole. Daisy barks on the deck above. Fouché points the gun at Liz.

"You know, Liz, you keep fucking up my scapegoats. Why did you have to kill Timmons? If you had just arrested him, he would have denied it but you would have made him wear it. It made perfect sense—the Stanley Park Rapist was also the Foot Killer. We even had Rosie George baiting the public with the theory. But *nooo*, you and Jack had to go all cowboy on his ass."

He scratches his lower leg again. "Jack is good though. Alcoholic ex-cop with a history of violence. Shot a man in cold blood. He and I have very similar profiles, you know."

"Except Jack's not a psychopath."

Fouché shrugs. "Let's not quibble about details. It was easy to keep track of both of you through your mobile phone. Did the same thing to Amanda."

"You cloned my phone."

"Liz, cloning is so twentieth century. There's an app for that now. For just $4.99 you can download spyware that quietly forwards all your calls, e-mails and texts. I did it when I broke into your car. I installed one on Timmons' phone too. I love technology. Planting the knife was just an insurance policy. Worked out better than I planned."

Fouché props his foot up on the settee and rubs his leg.

"Don't know why this leg gets itchy."

Fouché pulls up his pant leg. With a quick click of a button, he calmly slips off a state-of-the-art, carbon-fiber and vinyl, prosthetic foot.

Liz backs up a step, bumps into the companionway ladder beside the galley stove. Trying to catch her breath in the suddenly thick and airless atmosphere.

Fouché vigorously scratches the air below his stump, where his phantom foot should be, like a dog air-scratching with its hind leg. Rain pounds down on the deck above.

"What?" says Fouché. "You've never seen a guy with a prosthetic before?"

Fouché stops scratching. He holds up his complex prosthetic foot.

"I know. I have, like, the BMW of prosthetics, courtesy of an Al-Qaeda IED and the Canadian taxpayer. You wouldn't believe the advancements in biomechanics and dynamic responsive limbs. Most people can't even see a limp. I almost went running with you. Anyhow, the thing is, Liz, people just assume the feet get cut off postmortem, but what's the fun in that? Mine wasn't."

"You freaky fucking bastard."

"You should have heard Richards squeal like a little girl. And Amanda . . . Amanda was . . . *exquisite*. Some of my best work. The look in her eyes when she knew what was about to happen. And there was not a *damn thing* she could do about it. Well, you know, you saw the tape. She was so beautiful. I never molested any of them. I didn't have to. It was transcendent. Better than sex. Much better. I'm not a rapist, for God's sake."

"Why did you kill Knifeblade and Richards?"

"I know. Kind of off my profile, I do prefer blondes. Bob was unlucky, wrong place, wrong time. He couldn't live after he saw Amanda in the boat. I just had time to dump his body. And Richards . . . Don't you see, I killed him for you, Liz. That and he found my boathouse."

"He was a good man."

"He was a sexist, old-school, washed-out pain in the ass. When he found out Timmons wasn't Amanda's ex, he wouldn't let it go. He said he didn't like the goddamn *timeline*. And he insisted on trying to find Amanda's ex-boyfriend. I told him to let it go but he said he had a 'hunch.' He'd no idea his partner actually *was* Amanda's ex-boyfriend." He laughs. "Like Richards said, 'It's always the boyfriend.'"

Daisy barks again from the deck. She tries to make her way down the steep ladder but is scared of the drop.

"Shut up! Fucking dog. Where was I?"

"Somewhere between bat-shit crazy and stark raving mad."

Fouché looks at his dart gun. "That's right. You know, the real trouble with these dart guns is you can't regulate the dosage. Too little, they wake up before I can get them tied down. Too much, you kill them right away. And *that's* no fun."

"You know the other trouble with dart guns, Doug?" says Liz calmly, looking him in the eye. "They only hold one dart."

Liz throws the hot coffee pot at Fouché's face, launching herself at him. Fouché screams, but recovers. They grapple, a brutal struggle at close quarters, banging around in the little cabin. Fouché turns her and slams her head into the mast step, making her see stars, darkness rippling in for a terrifying moment. Daisy jumps down the ladder and bites Fouché's stump. He kicks her away. Daisy yelps. But the distraction Daisy creates is enough for Liz to grab Knifeblade's knife off the table. Fouché draws his RCMP service pistol and fires, just missing Liz as she stabs him in the chest—but only an inch or so of the blade penetrates. He screams in pain, fires again, wide, drops the pistol, grabs the knife and Liz's hands but Liz has the leverage and the advantage.

She bears down. "You know, Fouché, the great thing about knives—you never run out of bullets."

Fouché's eyes widen suddenly as she shoves the knife deeper into his chest. "They are precise." She shoves the knife another inch. "The purity of steel." She shoves it deeper as Fouché gags, spitting up blood. "And you know, I think Bob was right. At close quarters, I'd take a knife over a gun any day."

Liz takes back her right fist and hammers it home, shoving the blade in all the way up to the hilt. Fouché gasps, keels over, eyes wide-open, blood running from his mouth. She kicks away his service pistol, rolls him over and checks his pulse to confirm that he is dead, wiggles the knife. His eyes are beginning to glaze over. She sits slumped beside Fouché on the cabin sole for a long moment, then, feeling ancient and exhausted, her limbs weighing a ton, she moves to Jack and tries to revive him. He's alive, but still out cold. Liz fumbles for the mike and gets on the radio, tunes to Emergency Channel 16.

"May Day. May Day. May Day. This is the sailing yacht *Skookum*. We are in Waterfall Cove in Desolation Sound, about fifteen miles north of Lund, and need emergency assistance. This is an RCMP emergency. May Day! May Day!"

31

Liz has managed to get Jack into a sitting position at the settee. As he starts to come around, she hands Jack a cup of coffee from a fresh pot to wake him up from the tranquilizer. Daisy is seated by his side, whimpering softly. Fouché's body is still slumped over on the cabin sole.

"Christ. That dart really has me looped." He looks her in the eye. "Liz, thanks. Now I owe *you* one."

"Let's just call it even."

"Did you seriously think I did it?"

"I didn't know what to think . . . But how else could you have come across Bob's one-of-a-kind knife?"

"Fouché planted it, obviously. Besides, I told you, serial killers don't have dogs."

"Is that vintage Sherlock Holmes?"

"No that's vintage Jack Harris."

Daisy licks his hand.

"Do you forgive me?" says Liz. "For not trusting you?"

"Yes. Of course."

The boat makes a sudden lurch in the shifting wind. Fouché's body moves, a gurgle of air escapes his lips. Jack and Liz look at each other. Jack grabs Fouché's gun.

"Sure he's dead?"

Liz grabs the knife sticking out of Fouché's chest and gives it a hearty shake. Fouché's glassy eyes show nothing.

"You know what they say about us PR gals. We always get our man."

They hear the deep burbling sound of an approaching motorboat. A searchlight beam flashes through the portholes, lighting up the ghastly scene with a blue glow for an instant. A disembodied and alien voice echoes across the cove.

"This is Coast Guard Canada! Prepare to be boarded! *C'est la Garde côtière du Canada! Préparez-vous à être arraisonnés!*"

■ ■ ■

The red Coast Guard RIB Zodiac navigates the narrow entrance to Waterfall Cove, shining its searchlight through the gloom, the beam playing on the only boat in the anchorage. *Skookum* is a small dot of light in a huge wilderness of water, timber, mountains and twilight.

AUTHORS' NOTE AND ACKNOWLEDGEMENTS

This book is a work of fiction and characters and some places have been invented. However, the severed feet mystery is real. Since 2007, fifteen human feet (not including hoaxes) have been found along the shores of British Columbia and Washington State. The RCMP, one of the finest law enforcement organizations in the world, attributes these feet to unknown suicides and resolutely states "there is no sign of foul play". The mystery remains unsolved.The authors gratefully wish to acknowledge and thank the following people for their valuable assistance and insightful editorial advice: Alex Butler, Richard Berger, Chris Chesser, Mark McIntire, Denis O'Neill and Eduardo Rossoff.

Fraser Heston would also like to thank his wife Marilyn Heston, Michelle MacLaren, and Vincent Massey for introducing him to the mystical waters of Desolation Sound.

For more information please visit:
www.desolationsoundnovel.com

Made in the USA
San Bernardino, CA
11 September 2019